# Dave

# At Singapore

# *by* R. Sidney Bowen

Author of

**"Dave Dawson at Dunkirk"**

**"Dave Dawson with the R.A.F."**

**"Dave Dawson on Convoy Patrol"**

**"Dave Dawson Flight Lieutenant**

The Saalfield publishing company

Akron, Ohio

New York

Republished, and reedited from the public domain.

**ISBN-13:
978-1522901822**

**ISBN-10:
1522901825**

## CONTENTS

# CHAPTER ONE
## *Eastward to War*

Freddy Farmer leaned against the bow rail of the British Cruiser Harkness and stared intently at the greenish brown line that was landfall low down on the distant horizon.

"Singapore!" he breathed presently in almost a tone of awe. "Singapore! The place of ten thousand mysteries."

Dave Dawson standing at his elbow chuckled softly and gave a half nod of his head.

"Right, my little man," he said. "And the place of ten thousand smells, too, according to what fellows have told me who've been there."

Young Farmer groaned and gave his American pal a scornful look.

"You would say something like that," he grunted. "Hard hearted to the core, that's you. No wonder you're the terror of the Nazi pilots. You've no romance in your soul, Dave. Absolutely none at all. Now, take Singapore. It's...."

"You take it," Dawson interrupted. "Matter of fact, it was your idea in the first place. There we were, nicely settled in good old England, and what do you do but up and get itchy wings. And so here we are, three weeks later, practically over on the other side of the world. You sure do like to get around, I'll say!"

The English youth's eyes snapped fire as he faced Dawson straddle legged and arms akimbo.

"Well, bless my sainted aunt!" he exploded. "Listen to who's talking! I simply told you there was a rumor going around that Fighter pilots could put in requests for transfer to other theatres of war, now that Jerry wasn't sending so many wings over England. It was *you*, my good man, who went to the Group Commander and checked the rumor. And it was *you* who put in a request that we *both* go to the Far East Fleet Air Arm. Deny that, Dave Dawson, and over the side you go! And in case you don't know it, there are a lot of man-eating sharks in these waters!"

"Okay, okay!" Dawson cried and threw up both hands in a token of surrender. "But I only did it because I thought you'd enjoy the trip and the new scenery. Anyway, there's your mysterious Singapore ... unless the navigation officer aboard this battle wagon has got his calculations all messed up."

"I accept your humble apology," Farmer said and grinned. "So, we'll say no more about it. There's one thing, though, Dave. Why did you pick the Far East for us? There's no action out here, save hunting down a U-boat and a surface raider now and then."

"No?" Dawson grunted scornfully and pointed a hand toward the north. "Well, a couple of thousand miles up that way there's a group of islands that are called Japan. It's full of a mess of little brown rats that even their bucktoothed Emperor Hirohito wouldn't trust any farther than he could throw an aircraft carrier. And in case you haven't been reading the newspapers for the last two or three years, Japan is a member of the Axis. The other two members are Germany and Italy. No charge for the information, my little man."

"Well, thank goodness you've told me!" Freddy Farmer snapped. "It would be terrible to go on being so ignorant for the rest of my life. All right, so Japan is up north. What of it? Do you think they'd be mad enough to attempt to attack the British Naval Base at Singapore? It would be sheer madness. Suicide for the whole blasted lot of them."

"Sweet tripe!" Dawson groaned. "So you've been believing that junk, too?"

"What junk?" the English youth demanded.

"The stuff the so called military experts put in the papers, and blat out over the radio," Dawson said. "Look, as war veterans go, I'm just as wet behind the ears as the next fellow. But there is one thing that my war experiences, such as they've been, have taught me."

"Ah, more wisdom!" Farmer breathed. "Tell me. I can hardly wait, Professor!"

"Okay, funny boy," Dawson said gravely. "It is simply this, and you can take it or leave it, for all I care. But ever since Hitler's bums marched into Poland the thing that everybody believed was impossible to do was just what the enemy went out *and did*! Well, am I right or wrong?"

The English youth didn't reply for a moment or so. He turned forward and stared at the distant horizon. The Harkness was cutting through the sun flooded waters of the China Sea at a fast clip, and the greenish-brown coastline was now well up above the level of the sea. The peaks of Malay mountains could be seen against the clear blue sky, and a little to the south was another mark on the horizon that was the Dutch owned island of Sumatra. The approaches to Singapore! A sight that one could view a million times and still be eager for another look. The Far East! Mystery, romance, treachery, and death. It all depended upon what you wanted ... and upon how you went about finding it!

Freddy Farmer shook his head as though to break the spell that gripped his thoughts and his imagination. He turned back to Dawson, and his face was grave, and his clear eyes serious.

"Yes, you're quite right, Dave," he said quietly. "The blasted enemy really has beaten us to it every time, and done the very thing we didn't even dream he would try. Then you mean...? You look for Japan to declare war against us here in the Far East, and have a go at Singapore?"

"Hey, hold everything, pal!" Dawson said with a laugh. "I'm no crystal ball gazer, and I haven't got a single secret agent in the Jap Emperor's palace. I don't know a thing. I've just got a hunch that...."

"Good Lord, Dawson, hunches again!" Farmer groaned. "I might have known it would work up to that."

"So it's a hunch!" Dave growled as his ears got red. "But my hunches haven't all been strike-outs in the past, I might remind you. Take that time in Libya...."

"Spare me!" Farmer cried. "Didn't I have to live through it with you? Wasn't that punishment enough for my sin of knowing you? But go on with what you meant to say."

"Why do I waste breath on dumb bunnies!" Dawson sighed. "Well, anyway, I figure the picture this way. Hitler got England's front door slammed hard on his fingers when he tried to push it open last year. In Russia the Jerries are right now receiving the biggest surprise of this war. They're getting the pants shot off them just when they thought they were going to have breakfast, lunch, and dinner in the Kremlin, in Moscow. And in Libya the Wops and the Jerries are setting all kinds of new Olympic distance records trying to get away from our boys out there. So, what's left? The Far East. That means Japan. I've a hunch that the Japs are only waiting for the right moment to jump. Sure, I may be all wet, and the Japs may stay in their holes. But, I've got the hunch that they won't. So.... Hey! What am I doing all this talking for, anyway!"

"The old American custom of letting off steam, I fancy," Freddy Farmer said with a chuckle. "However, I'd not be too surprised if you were right. The blasted Japs are...."

The English youth cut himself off short as a young pink cheeked naval lieutenant came up to them and saluted smartly.

"Captain Standers' compliments," he said. "He wishes to see you in his quarters at once."

Both Dawson and Farmer nodded, then looked questioningly at each other as the junior naval rating did a snappy about face and walked away.

"The Old Man wants us?" Freddy murmured. "What for, I wonder?"

"Search me," Dawson said with a shrug. Then with a quick side glance at his pal, "Unless it's for the usual thing."

"Usual thing?" Freddy Farmer echoed sharply. "Just what do you mean?"

Dawson jerked his head at the swiftly approaching shoreline.

"We're getting close to port, and will be going ashore soon," he said. "I suppose the Skipper wants to lay down the law to you, as usual. And get me to promise to keep an eye on you ... as usual. Well, there's one way to find out. That's to go see him. Come along, my little man."

Dawson turned, took one step, tripped over a foot that shot out suddenly, and went flat on his face.

"Sorry, old thing," Freddy murmured, innocent eyed. "Was my foot in your way, by any chance?"

Dave got slowly to his feet, brushed off his uniform and glanced down over the side of the cruiser. He sighed and shook his head.

"What's the sense?" he growled. "The sharks would probably throw you right back aboard!"

## CHAPTER TWO
### *Strange Orders*

Captain Standers, commander of the Harkness, was a true type of British sea dog in both stature and looks. His legs were as sturdy and stubby as fire hydrants. His body was like a barrel, and two muscle bulging arms hung from a pair of shoulders as broad as the back of a taxi cab. His face was lined and wrinkled from countless hours on the bridge in fair weather and bad. And it was the color of well tanned saddle leather, save a spot on each cheek that was apple red. The eyes were small and set wide apart, but in their depths was a glint that gave you the feeling the man could see right through six inch steel armor. All in all, Captain Standers looked quite capable of leaping overboard and shoving his cruiser back into deep water should it ever run aground.

He swept the two R.A.F. youths with his gimlet eyes as they entered his quarters and saluted.

"At ease, Gentlemen," he said in a voice that could double for a foghorn. "Be seated. It seems that news of your coming to Singapore has traveled ahead of you. I have a wireless, here, from Air Vice Marshal Bostworth, of Singapore Air Base. He has made a request regarding you two."

"Air Vice Marshal Bostworth, of Singapore Base!" Dawson gasped as the Cruiser's captain paused for breath. "But there must be some mistake, sir. I mean, we saw Air Vice Marshal Bostworth just before we left England. It was he who okayed our request for transfer to duty with the Far East Fleet Air Arm."

Captain Standers snorted softly and gave Dawson a look as though he were some school kid who had fumbled his homework.

"Quite, Flight Lieutenant," he said. "But we've been at sea close to three weeks. It's quite possible to *fly* from London to Singapore, via Egypt, in less than half that time."

"Yes, sir, of course," Dave murmured as his face burned. "I.... Well, it sort of startled me, sir."

9

"Quite so," the Harkness' commander grunted. "That is neither here nor there, however. The wireless is from Air Vice Marshal Bostworth, and it was sent from R.A.F. Base at Singapore. The request is for you two pilots to take one of the Harkness' planes aloft and cruise over the Singapore Strait for two hours and then proceed to the R.A.F. Base on the Island. Air Vice Marshal Bostworth will meet you there. You've got that all clear?"

Freddy and Dave looked at each other, and their thoughts were identical. Was somebody trying to kid somebody, or something? Why in the world were they to take one of the Harkness' Bristol powered Fairey "Swordfishes" aloft and use up gas and oil for an hour or two? Why not go right on into the Johore Strait Naval Anchorage aboard the Harkness, and then step ashore to meet the Air Vice Marshal? It certainly didn't make sense, and the bewildered look that spread over each youth's face said as much to Captain Standers. He shrugged and made a little gesture with his hand.

"Don't bother asking me questions," he said. "I haven't the faintest idea what the answers should be. Sounds like so much R.A.F. rubbish, I fancy. However, the request has the approval of the Base Admiral, so there's only one thing I can do about it. Assign you to one of our planes, and let you go your way."

"Begging your pardon, sir," Freddy Farmer spoke up, his face slightly crimson, "but was that all to the message? Just that we go aloft and spend two hours in the air before landing at Singapore R.A.F. Base?"

"That was all, definitely," the Cruiser's captain replied. "As a matter of fact, I didn't believe it myself and had the first message checked. The repeat was the same, however. Also, both messages were in a new emergency code. You say you saw Air Vice Marshal Bostworth just before you left England?"

"Yes, sir," the boys replied in one voice.

"I see," the senior officer murmured. Then flinging them a keen look, "He didn't mention anything about coming out to Singapore himself? Didn't say he might have a job for you two to do out here? The three of us know that Air Vice Marshal Bostworth is connected with Air Intelligence. And, naturally, your service records are not exactly deep dark secrets. You aren't, perhaps, as ignorant of what all this crazy business means as you appear to be, eh?"

The two R.A.F. pilots grinned, but they both shook their heads.

"Sorry, sir, but it's as much of a mystery to us," Freddy Farmer spoke for them. "Air Vice Marshal Bostworth didn't even give us an inkling that he might be coming out here. It really is surprising news to us, sir."

Captain Standers hesitated as though about to speak, then thought better of it and pushed up onto his feet.

"Well, one can't know about everything in this blasted war, I fancy," he grunted. "You two had better get on with it. Use the plane on Catapult Number Three. I've already told the signal officer to make ready. Good luck. And, by the way!"

"Yes, sir?" the two pilots murmured as the Cruiser's commander paused and scowled at his gnarled hands.

"When you finally land at Singapore R.A.F. Base," he finally said, "please mention to Air Vice Marshal Bostworth that I'd jolly well like to have the plane back before we put to sea again. Planes are hard enough to get as it is. Well, luck to you anyway."

Some twenty minutes later Dave Dawson and Freddy Farmer were seated in a pontoon fitted, Bristol Pegasus engined Fairey "Swordfish" mounted on the starboard launching arm of Number Three catapult. The engine was ticking over and the Signal Officer standing on the flight bridge was ready to "shoot" the plane off into the air as soon as Dave at the controls gave him the signal.

Checking his engine instruments for the last time, the Yank R.A.F. ace turned in the seat and looked back at his English pal.

"All set for the mystery ride, Freddy?" he called out.

Young Farmer made a face and nodded.

"Let her go, Dave," he replied. "But I certainly hope these two hours whizz by, so's we can land at Singapore Base and find out what in the world this all means!"

"You and me both!" Dave grunted. "I've been given a lot of screwy orders in my time, but this one is certainly tops. Oh, well, we'll get a nice look at this neck of the Far East, anyway. Okay! Hold your hat. The balloon's going up!"

Turning front, Dave nodded to the waiting signal officer, and automatically braced his body and put his head firmly against the back rest, so that it wouldn't be snapped back when the launching "trigger" was pulled. A couple of seconds later the Swordfish's engine was roaring out its mighty song of power and straining at the locking-dogs that held it on the catapult arm. Another second and it was as though an invisible giant had slammed the rear end of the plane with the side of a barn door, or something. The Swordfish leaped forward like a scared cat. It shot off the end of the catapult arm, sank toward the water for a brief instant, then rose upward as the whirling prop bit into the air and produced flying speed.

Once clear and curving upward, Dave throttled slightly and held the nose on a gentle climb toward Heaven. He turned and grinned at Freddy and then glanced down back at the Harkness cutting through the sun flooded waters of the China Sea like a perfectly streamlined battle grey fish. For a moment signal flags that spelled out G-O-O-D L-U-C-K fluttered in the wind, then they were hauled down and the Harkness began falling far astern of the climbing plane. Dave looked front again, leveled off at a comfortable six thousand feet and relaxed comfortably in the seat.

"Ladies and Gentlemen!" came Freddy Farmer's voice to his ears. "On the far left you have the British owned island of Singapore. Just above it is the Malay Peninsula where they produce about eighty per cent of all the rubber in the world. And tin, also. A bit more to the north is French Indo-China. Far to the right are the Philippines. And way in back of you are the Dutch East Indies, including Borneo and Sumatra. If you smoke cigars, Ladies and Gentlemen, you should be doubly interested in Sumatra because the famous Sumatra leaf used as an outside wrapper for many, many brands of cigars comes from Sumatra. Personally, I'm not very interested because I do not smoke cigars. However...."

"However, shut up, Professor!" Dave interrupted with a laugh. "We can see it all, and we studied all about these parts when we were in school. But ... there is one question I would like to ask the learned Professor."

"Certainly, my child, certainly," Freddy Farmer replied. "Go right ahead. What do you want to know?"

"Boy, are you sticking your chin out!" Dave chuckled. "Okay! Why *are* we flying around up here, Professor?"

"Good Lord, I should have suspected that!" Freddy Farmer groaned. "Well, it's a secret. A very deep dark secret. Only one man knows. And so far he hasn't told anybody. He.... Hey, Dave!"

"Don't shout, I haven't jumped out, yet," Dave cried and turned quickly around. "What...?"

Dave stopped short and stared hard at his pal. Freddy Farmer was leaning way forward to the right and gaping puzzle eyed down at the rolling surface of the China Sea far ahead. He didn't switch his gaze to Dave's face. He simply made a little movement with one hand and kept his eyes riveted on something ahead.

"Take a look way out there, Dave!" he shouted. "I thought I saw some flashes of light."

"Light?" Dawson echoed sharply. "This time of day? Are you nuts, or just seeing things?"

"I saw something!" the English youth said. "At least I'd be willing to swear to it. Sort of flashes of light, as though some surface ship were signaling by mirror. You know, by heliograph."

Dave didn't make any comment to that for a moment or two. He had turned front and was sweeping the waters ahead and below with his eyes. However, that was all he saw. Just a limitless expanse of robin's egg blue water that was streaked and smeared with the gold of the blazing sun. True, the rays of the sun bouncing off the rolling blue swells seemed to shower up clusters of golden specks in all directions that dazzled his eyes. But no matter how hard he strained his eyes he could see not the slightest sign of a surface ship, to say nothing of the telltale ribbon of smoke trailing back from her stacks. Eventually he gave it up and turned to look at his pal again.

"Is this some kind of a gag?" he demanded. "Or did you really see something? Maybe it was just sunbeams dancing off the water, huh?"

Freddy Farmer wiped a hand across his eyes, sighed and shrugged.

"Maybe," he said in a puzzled voice. "But, if so, it's the first time I ever saw sunbeams send out dots and dashes."

"Dots and dashes?" Dave echoed. "Did you catch any of them? The letters, I mean?"

"Too fast," Freddy said with a shake of his head. "And what little I did catch didn't mean any letters in the Morse Code. But ... maybe I was just seeing things. Sorry."

Dave grinned and winked, and turned front once more.

"Think nothing of it, my little pal," he said. "Even the best of us make mistakes now and...."

Dave clamped his lips shut on the last, sat up straight in the seat and stared hard down at the water to his right and some four or five miles away. Perhaps it actually was a sunbeam dancing back up at him, but for a brief instant he was certain he had seen four or five rapid flashes of light down on the surface of the water. Another moment and he was positive beyond all shadow of a doubt. There was a light flashing down there on the water. Rather it was the reflection of the sun's rays on a heliograph mirror. However, the flashes were both long and short, and Dave didn't have to look twice to realize perfectly well that some kind of a message was being flashed from down there on the water.

"But how, and who's doing it?" Dave gulped out the question aloud. "Unless I'm completely nuts, or stone blind, there's nothing but water down there. Hey, Freddy!"

"Yes, I see it, too," the English youth spoke up. "Thought I'd let you see it for yourself this time. What do you make of it, Dave? A bit weird, isn't it?"

"And a lot more than that!" Dave grunted and was uncomfortably conscious of an eerie tingling at the back of his neck. "I don't see a darn thing else but water and that flashing light. Hey! Do you suppose it could be a sheet of metal, or something, that's being caught by the sun as it rides those swells?"

"It could be, but I'm sure it isn't!" Freddy Farmer replied in a tight voice. "Dave, those are real dot and dash signals. Three dots—two dashes, then one dot and four dashes. Neither of those are Morse Code letters. Or International Morse, either. But, I'll eat my parachute pack if those aren't some kind of signals."

"Check and double check!" Dave grunted and scowled.

On impulse he took his eyes off the strange flashing signals far below and ahead, and twisting all the way around in the seat he took a good look at the surrounding heavens. Finally, he lowered his eyes to meet Freddy Farmer's puzzled gaze.

"Notice something else, Freddy, that seems to be a little out of whack?" he asked.

The English born R.A.F. ace took a quick look around, and shook his head.

"Can't say I do," he said. "Unless you mean us tooting around up here for no apparent reason ... at least, not to us. Why? What do you mean?"

Dave made a little gesture with one hand that included a sweep of the surrounding air.

"Just that," he said. "Full of nothing but sky and air. How come? How come we're the only plane that's burning gas and oil in these parts? Why isn't there a sign of any Singapore Base planes out on patrol? Particularly the U-boat patrol planes. Don't they care any more if supply ships heading for Singapore get torpedoed? In short, where is everybody?"

"By jove, that's right, Dave!" Freddy Farmer breathed with a catch in his voice. "Of course, they may have scared U-boats and surface raiders away from here for good, yet.... Yet you'd think they'd still maintain some kind of daylight patrol just in case."

"Took the words right out of my mouth," Dawson said with a grave nod. "Of course, it is the month of December, and maybe they've declared a truce out here until Xmas comes and goes. But it's darn queer. No planes in the air. No ships on the water. Even the Harkness is out of sight, now. Just us."

"And those queer light flashes down there," Freddy Farmer added. "Dave! I think we should...."

"Doggone right!" Dave cut in and shoved the stick forward. "We'll take us a better look anyway. Hang on, pal! These Swordfish jobs lose altitude in plenty hurry!"

Dave Dawson

---

## CHAPTER THREE
### *The Voice of Doom*

---

Dave wasn't kidding when he said that an aerial torpedo carrying Fairey Swordfish can go down in a hurry. The plane streaked seaward like a meteor in high gear. Dave held it in its steep dive until the rolling blue swells of the China sea came rushing up a little too close for comfort. Skillfully working the controls, he leveled off and shot the plane forward toward the spot where they had first noticed the weird flashes of light.

There were no flashes of light to be seen now, however. There was nothing but sun flooded rolling water. Dave stared hard, and so did Freddy Farmer, too. But it was just a waste of eyesight for all the good it did them.

"That makes us nuts, Freddy!" Dave sang out. "I don't see a thing, do you?"

"Not a thing!" Freddy called to him. "I fancy it must have been the sun's rays playing tricks on the water."

"Well, some trick, is all I've got to say," Dave grunted and climbed the Swordfish slightly for a better look. "The same combinations of dots and dashes were repeated over and over again."

"I know," Freddy said. "Like a blasted call signal on the short-wave radio. If they'd been different and jumbled up then you could put it down to sunlight bouncing off the water, but ... *Dave!* To the left! To the left! See that spot of white water? Foam? Dave! There's something there!"

Dave had already snapped his eyes to the left and was staring at a patch of foamy white water on the surface of the seemingly limitless stretch of rolling blue. The white foamy patch was there for a very good reason. It was the telltale wake left by a diving submarine. And even as Dave realized that he caught sight of a long cigar shaped shadow sliding forward just under the surface of the water.

"That's a submarine, Dave!" Freddy Farmer's excited voice confirmed Dawson's belief at practically the same instant. "It was on the surface and signalling us, but we couldn't see anything but the flash signals."

"Sure, so what?" Dave growled and veered the Swordfish around toward the shadow of the undersea craft. "But why signal *us*? And, also, why signal us and then dive when we start to come down? Our markings are plain enough."

"Maybe it's a German U-boat!" Freddy cried excitedly.

"Maybe," Dave said with a shrug. "But it still doesn't make sense. *Why* was the guy signalling to us?"

"Maybe he wasn't signalling to us," Freddy Farmer ventured.

Dave snorted and made a little gesture with his free hand.

"Then who was he signalling to?" he demanded. "The man in the moon above us? I took a good look, Freddy. I'll swear on a ten foot stack of bibles that we're the only plane aloft in these parts. No, that underwater boat was signalling to us, and...."

He left the rest hanging in midair as he suddenly saw the moving shadow of the submarine grow clearer and clearer as it rose to the surface. A moment later the surface of the blue water boiled white and the conning tower mast and hatch rose up into view. Another moment and the whole bridge and decks were awash. Like a man in a dream Dave blinked his eyes at the strange sight. It was a submarine sure enough, but it was of a type he had never seen in his life. And what was even more astonishing, it was painted a dull greenish blue to make it blend in well nigh perfectly with the surrounding waters.

"Good Lord!" Freddy Farmer gasped. "What is it? Nazi, or one of our new types? And look at those two bow guns, Dave. And.... Dave! Look at those seamen spill out of that opened conning tower hatch! They're coming out like blasted rabbits. Get closer to the thing. It's like something out of a fairy story book."

Dave Dawson only half heard his friend's exclamations, for all of his attention and his eyes were fixed on the strange craft just off and below the left wings. Just as Freddy Farmer had said, the figures of seamen were popping out of the opened conning tower hatch like rabbits out of a hat. They looked neither German nor English. They were all short and stocky, and they moved about as though operated by strings held by invisible hands.

Wide eyed, Dave stared at them; watched them pop out and go scrambling down the bridge ladder and forward toward the bow. And then things happened so fast that both Dave and Freddy were too stunned and paralyzed to even think, let alone move. The two forward guns were swung around toward them, covers were ripped off, and in the next instant the muzzle of each gun belched out smoke and flame, and the Swordfish heeled over drunkenly on the opposite wings as though it had crashed full out into an invisible brick wall suspended in the sky.

A thousand steel fists hammered against Dave's body and his brain became filled with flashing white light. As though from a million miles away he heard the wild, excited yells from Freddy Farmer's lips. He heard also the scream of the Bristol Pegasus engine over-revving. And, although he was not conscious of doing so, he reached out and cut the ignition and hauled back the throttle with a single movement of his hand.

Then, just as suddenly as the flashing white light had filled his brain, the light disappeared, and he realized that the plane was cutting crazily down sidewise toward the rolling blue swells that were now perilously close. The engine cowling looked as though it had been hit by a twenty-ton tank. The metal was hanging in gleaming ribbons. And as for the engine itself, one whole side of the powerful radial engine was just so much mangled junk.

Sight and action became one for Dave. Even as he saw what the exploding shell from the mysterious submarine's gun had done, he slammed on opposite control hard and slowly got the Swordfish back onto even keel. But shell fragments had parted a couple of the cables and no sooner was the plane on even keel than it struggled to slump down by the wing again. As a matter of fact, had the water not been but inches from the bottom of the pontoon, and Dave able to sit down quickly, the plane would have cartwheeled over and gone in wingtips first to really crack up. As it was, the hasty emergency landing made Dave's teeth click, and his backbone to feel as though it had been snapped off in half a dozen places. However, the plane stayed put on its pontoon, and in a couple of seconds the stars and comets ceased dancing around inside Dave's head.

The first thing he did was to twist his head around and look for the strange submarine. But it wasn't anywhere to be seen. It had obviously crash-dived once the Swordfish had been hit. There wasn't even the froth of its wake to be seen. Dave took a good look in all directions, and then looked at Freddy Farmer's wide eyed and slightly pale face. He grinned and touched a finger to his flying helmet.

"Weren't in a hurry to get any place, were you, boss?" he called out. "I think we've had an accident. In fact, I'm cockeyed sure of it, boss."

The kidding words snapped the strain that was gripping the English youth. Freddy slowly relaxed, swallowed a couple of times, and then matched Dave's grin.

"It doesn't matter, driver," he said. Then with a wave of his hand, "Welcome to Singapore. Nice place, isn't it?"

"Oh, jolly, as the beef eating English say," Dave mimicked with a chuckle. "A trifle on the wet side, though. You okay, Freddy?"

"My heart's stuck fast against my back teeth," the other said. "I fancy, though, it'll drop back into place in a moment. But that was the damnedest ever, Dave. What in the world do you think?"

Dave gave a shake of his head and heaved a long puzzled sigh.

"I can't even try to guess, much less think," he finally grunted. "Thank the gods that only one shell hit us ... and it on the nose. About ten feet farther back and you and I would be going places right now full of slivers of steel. What do you think?"

"Less than that, I'm afraid," Freddy said, and cast anxious eyes about the surface of the surrounding water. "To tell the truth, I feel like I've just awakened from a horrible nightmare."

"Take a look at our engine!" Dave growled. "It was no nightmare, son. Say, Freddy. You won't laugh, will you?"

"Lord knows I could do with a good laugh right now," the English youth said and unbuckled his uncomfortable parachute harness. "But what's on your mind? I promise not to laugh."

"Those guys who came popping out on that sub's deck like rabbits," Dave said after a long frowning pause. "Know what they looked like to me?"

"What?"

"Like Japs," Dave said, straight faced.

Freddy Farmer gulped and blinked. It was a couple of seconds before he could get his tongue to form the word.

"Japs?" he gasped.

"Sure, Japs," Dave repeated. "You know, short for Japanese. I'll bet you that was a Jap submarine, and those guys who let fly at us were Japs."

The English youth pondered over that a moment, and meanwhile kept up his nervous-eyed search of the surrounding rolling swells.

"They did have the Japanese build, I'll admit," he finally said. "But.... Lord! It's fantastic, Dave! Why in the world would a Jap submarine come to the surface and blast away at us? We're not even carrying a torpedo, to say nothing of bombs."

"But we are carrying a two-way radio," Dave pointed out gravely. "It could be that they didn't want anybody to know they were this close to Singapore. They didn't hear us use the radio, so decided to surprise us and blast us before we could use it. I only hope they don't surface again and make sure with those bow guns. Say! What are you hunting for anyway?"

"What do you think?" Freddy Farmer snapped. "I'm hoping they *don't* come back to the surface, either. That they'll believe they got us with that one blast. But, Dave, it's still fantastic. England's not at war with Japan. Standers of the Harkness would have been informed if war was declared while we were at sea. And he certainly would have told his officers."

"You and your English rules of war!" Dave groaned. "Look, little man, they don't *declare* war any more these days. You only find out you're at war when you feel the pain of the knife going into your back. But I only said they *looked* like Japs. Maybe they weren't. Maybe they grow them that way in Hitlerland, now. Who can tell?"

"Well, I guess it doesn't make much difference who they were," Freddy said with a shrug. "The point is, *here* we are, and *what* are we going to do about it."

"We could swim," Dave grunted, "but I never was very good at making friends with man-eating sharks. If you must know the truth, I figure we've got to sit here and wait."

"But that might be forever!" Freddy cried in a startled voice.

"Yeah, a long time," Dave said, and tapped a finger to his head. "Stop wondering about the Japs, pal, and relax and use your brains. Or did you leave them in England?"

"Very funny!" Freddy growled. "But just what are you being so long winded about? Come on, spit it out!"

"What would you do without me always around to hold your hand, and dry your tears," Dave taunted with a grin. "We sit here until they come out and pick us up, of course."

"Until *they* come out?" Freddy echoed sharply. "Who knows where we...?"

He stopped short and made a face as though he had bitten his tongue. Then he grinned sheepishly as the flush came into his cheeks.

"Sorry, old thing," he mumbled. "Stupid of me, wasn't it? I see what you mean, of course. When Air Vice Marshal Bostworth doesn't see us return from a two hour mystery patrol over this area, he'll jolly well send out search planes, eh?"

"He'd jolly well better!" Dave grunted and fished for the chocolate bars he always carried. "Or I'll punch him right on the nose if I ever meet up with him again. He got us into this, and he can get us out! Here, have a hunk of chocolate. And don't chew with your mouth open. It's not nice, and it makes me nervous."

Freddy Farmer shrugged when he could think of no fitting retort to that one. However, he accepted one of the bars of chocolate, and both boys fell to eating and silently staring out over the expanse of rolling blue water that seemed to touch no land in any direction.

# CHAPTER FOUR
## *Satan over Singapore*

Exactly five hours later the two boys were still staring out across the rolling blue swells, and in between times they had searched and researched the blazing China Sea skies with their tired eyes. But from then until now they had seen nothing to bring joy or alarm to their hearts. No planes or ships had appeared, and although they had kidded and horsed around to keep each other's spirits at a high level, tiny fears, and dreads, and doubts, were little by little boring deeper into their thoughts. For five hours neither had seen the slightest sign of anything that might mean rescue. And for five solid hours each had expected the mysterious submarine to rise to the surface again and really finish them off. After all, they had been shot down by the undersea boat's guns for reasons they still couldn't figure out. But just to be shot down and left floating alive was something else again. That is, unless the crew and officers of that strange submarine were of the belief that they had died.

Licking his dry lips, Dave half turned in the seat and shot a quick glance back at Freddy Farmer. There was a set smile on the English youth's lips, but the tightness at the corners of his eyes, and a faint line of worry that creased his forehead told that the youth was struggling inwardly to keep control of his jangled nerves and not go haywire.

"I think I forgot to ask you," Dave said. "Just how did you like your visit to Singapore, anyway?"

"Top-hole!" Freddy said with a forced smile. "So ... so stimulating, and educational, you know. Fact is, I don't believe I'll ever forget it. One of the milestones in my life."

"Speaking of things educational," Dawson said to keep the conversation alive, "what do you know about Singapore, anyway?"

"Ask me, and find out, my little man," Freddy said with a little wave of his hand.

Dave dragged down the corners of his mouth, and squinted at his pal.

"A smart guy, huh?" he grunted. "Okay, I will ask you a few things. First, what does Singapore mean?"

"Don't you know?" Freddy retorted.

"Come on, none of that stuff!" Dave cried. "Stop crawling, young man. Tell teacher, or else admit you're dumb. What does Singapore mean?"

"Singapore means nothing!" Freddy shot at him. "It is the modern spelling of the city's real name centuries ago. Then it was Singhapura. That is a Sanskrit word that means City of the Lion."

Dave made a mock bow and went through the motions of tipping his hat.

"Well, knock me over with a Flying Fortress!" he exclaimed. "I guess the guy did spend two or three years in school. Okay, tell me some more, sonny."

"It's rather a nice sort of place, if you go in for that sort of place," Freddy said gravely. "It is an island, of course. It was picked as a British navy outpost by a Sir Stafford Raffles many, many years ago. It covers about two hundred and sixteen square miles and it guards the trade routes to the Indian Ocean. It is very well fortified, and any nation who tries to take it away from us is going to have a battle on his hands, I can tell you. The city is built...."

"Okay, okay!" Dave laughed and threw up his hands. "I guess you've read books. Spare me the rest of the details. I read a book once, myself."

"Right-o," Freddy Farmer said. "Now it's my turn to ask questions. No, not about Singapore. Here's a question that oddly enough not one man in fifty could answer correctly."

"Then shoot!" Dawson said with a chuckle. "Me, I'm that one man."

"Here goes then," the English born R.A.F. ace said. "Is there a type of Nazi dive bomber called the Stuka?"

Dave Dawson sat up a little straighter in the cockpit seat and gave his friend a keen look.

"What was that last one?" he demanded. "You wouldn't be kidding a pal, would you, pal?"

"Certainly not!" Freddy retorted. "And *you* stop crawling. Answer the question. Is there a type of Nazi dive bomber called the Stuka?"

"I hope to kiss a Messerschmitt there is!" Dave replied. "And I wish I had a dime for every time one of them has come piling down in my direction. What is this, anyway? You didn't drop your brains over the side, did you?"

"No, but you must have!" the English youth snapped back. "My poor misinformed little friend, Stuka is a name for *all* kinds of dive bombers. Not just one type, as is commonly believed. It comes from the German word *Sturzkampfflugzeug*. And that word means, plunge-battle-fight-apparatus. And so, I would suggest that you go back and make your solo flight all over again."

"My, my!" Dave breathed and gave a shake of his head in mock admiration. "After all this time and I didn't once dream that you had that big word inside of you. I must really get to know you one of these days. You'd be quite something to have along at one of those radio quiz programs. I just bet you got sore fingers from tearing off box tops, and sending into the corner drugstore. But hold it! You don't have advertising on your English radio programs, do you?"

"No, we don't," Freddy said with a frown. "And what do you mean, tear off a box top?"

"It's a radio stunt used back home to build up sales," Dave explained. "A manufacturer may be offering a booklet, or some kind of prize free, see? You can get it for nothing. All you do is buy say five or ten boxes of his product, tear off the tops and send them in with your name and address. And they send you whatever it is they are offering special, see? The catch is to get you to buy more of his product so's you can tear off the box tops. I once tried to get a book of old American songs that was being offered, but the folks wouldn't let me. It would have cost my Dad close to six thousand dollars to get the top of the boxes their product came in."

Freddy Farmer's eyes popped, and his mouth fell open.

"Six thousand dollars?" he gasped. "Good Lord! Why that much money?"

"The company sold pianos!" Dave said and ducked as Freddy flushed and swung his opened hand.

"When will I learn not to believe a thing that falls out of your big mouth!" Freddy groaned. Then after a moment's silence, he said, "This is a bit of foolishness, isn't it? Why don't we talk about what's really on our minds?"

"Okay," Dave said with a shrug. "Let's talk about it, then. Go ahead."

"Well, right at this moment I'm not feeling too kindly toward Air Vice Marshal Bostworth," Freddy said. "It's over three hours since we were to meet him at Singapore R.A.F. Base. I should think he would have sent planes out hunting for us by now. What do you think?"

Dave didn't answer for a moment. He slowly twisted around in the seat and took a good look at the sky and at the four horizons. He saw nothing in the air, and only far to the south did he see the thin dark line low down that marked land of some sort. It could be any one of the several islands that dotted the Strait.

"The same as you think, I guess, Freddy," he said presently, turning to his friend. "I frankly thought that we might have to wait for a spell or so. But not so long as this. If help's coming I hope it comes soon. That sun is getting closer and closer to the western horizon. Maybe when we didn't show up Air Vice Marshal Bostworth decided that Captain Standers wouldn't let us take a plane. And speaking of Standers, he's sure going to tear out his hair when he doesn't get this Fairey Swordfish back. He struck me as a lad who doesn't like folks to keep things they borrow."

"Oh, bother to Standers!" Freddy grunted and shook a hand impatiently. "What do we do when darkness falls, Dave?"

"Let it fall," the Yank replied. "What else?"

"Lord, what a help you are to a chap!" the English youth groaned. "We can't stay here forever. In case you don't realize it, my funny man, a seam has split in the pontoon, and we've been taking in water for an hour now. We're going to go under eventually."

"Yes, I've known we were taking in water, Freddy," Dave said quietly. "It isn't our combined weight that's making this job list a few degrees. But.... Well, Freddy, if it happens, I guess we've just got to take it, that's all. To tell the truth I've been beating my brains all over the place trying to figure some way to get in touch with the nearest shore. But the only way I can figure, wouldn't help us at all. Not unless help came out quicker than greased lightning."

"Well, as you've often said, anything's worth a try!" Freddy exclaimed. "What's your idea?"

"A bum one, and definitely out," Dave replied with a vigorous shake of his head. "The only way we could attract attention on shore is to set the plane on fire. If we did, it would only be a case of who got us first, the flames, or the sharks. Nope! I shouldn't even have brought it up."

"I'll say you shouldn't have!" Freddy growled and glared at the radio panel. "Look at that thing, there! Perfectly good when we're in the air but not worth a hoot down here on the water. Runs off the engine. Why don't they fit the things with hand driven generators so a chap can still work the radio when he's forced down?"

"They do on the big ships," Dave said. "But every extra pound of weight counts on this type of plane. Besides, Air Ministry expects you to be a good pilot and not get forced down."

"Blast Air Ministry!" Freddy snarled. "I wish some of those precious Brass Hats were here with us now. Perhaps they'd get a better idea of what a flying johnnie has to go through. It's all wrong, I tell you, Dave. The blokes at Air Ministry think that...."

"Tell me tomorrow, pal!" Dave suddenly broke in excitedly and flung up a hand toward the southwest. "Take a good look up there. Is that a plane, or have they got birds that big in this neck of the world?"

Freddy Farmer snapped his opened mouth shut and swiveled eagerly around in his seat, and peered intently in the direction of Dave's pointed finger. After a long minute he let clamped air out of his lungs in a great sigh of unbelievable relief.

"It's not a bird, Dave, it's a plane!" he cried. "A flying boat. It's one of our American built patrol Catalinas. Can't you recognize it? Lord knows you had enough experience on one!"[1]

"Old Freddy Farmer, the lad with telescopic eyes!" Dave cried as the prospect of immediate rescue drove all the little gnawing fears away. "They should get you to censor mail. You wouldn't have to take the letters out of the envelopes. But.... I hope you're right, sweetheart. I can see something headed this way, but it's too doggone small for a good look."

"Don't fret, it's a Catalina!" the English youth cried out happily. "I'm sure of it now. See? They've sighted us. They're coming down."

"They could be going out for lunch, for all I could tell," Dave grunted as he strained his eyes at the faint blackish blur high up in the China Sea sky. "But I'll take your word for it. Tell me, how many aboard? And has the pilot got a mustache or not?"

"He has not, but he's got a gold tooth!" Freddy snapped at him. "Stop pulling my leg. You must be able to see it clearly, now. Just because you're being rescued from a possible watery grave, my good man, don't be so blasted funny."

"Funny?" Dave echoed with a snort. "Look at me! I could weep with joy. Now that things look okay for us, I can admit that I was plenty worried awhile back. And no kidding, either!"

"Hardly the word to express how I felt," Freddy murmured and took a deep breath. "But perhaps we were really born under a lucky star, Dave. We always manage to skin through, somehow."

"Skin through, he says?" Dave echoed. "You mean, I walk through and pull you through after me. But let it go. Boy! What I'm going to tell Air Vice Marshal Bostworth when I see him!"

"Well, don't do it unless I'm outside the building," Freddy said.

"Outside the building?" Dave echoed and gave him a puzzled look. "Why?"

"To catch you when you come out," the English youth replied with a grin. "Air Vice Marshal Bostworth is six foot, three, as you know. And he is a holy terror about insubordination, as you *also* know."

"Yeah, that's true," Dave murmured, and watched the Catalina slide down lower and lower. "Well, at least I'll be thinking plenty when, and if, I meet him. Five hours on this sea of liquid fire is enough to make anybody sore. Okay, Freddy, give the pilot a wave. He's waving at us. Man, oh man! Doesn't it make you feel good to see that old R.A.F. insignia on the wings and hull?"

Freddy simply nodded. For the moment he was unable to speak. He was too choked up with emotion to dare trust his tongue. So he simply nodded, waved his hand and smiled all over the place as the Catalina sank lower, then cut around into the wind and made a feather-duster landing not over thirty yards to the lee of the slowly foundering Fairey Swordfish. Some clever sea rudder and engine throttling by the pilot soon brought the

Catalina close enough for the boys to catch the line that came singing out through the hull door. Another couple of moments and they were both way out on the Swordfish's left lower wing and scrambling aboard the Catalina.

"Dawson and Farmer, of course?" asked the sergeant gunner who helped them aboard.

"Check!" Dave gulped. "And were we glad to see this job. We were getting the feeling that we'd soon be food for those sharks that were gathering around."

"Nasty devils, those man eaters in these waters, sir," the Sergeant said, and stepped around Dave. "Stand clear, sir. I'm tossing a little time bomb into the Fairey. No sense having it float around for some johnny to run into. There! There we are."

A pang of sadness touched Dave's heart as he watched the small time bomb arc from the Sergeant's hand and plop down into the cockpit of the Fairey Swordfish. True, the seaplane was a total loss. The engine was a tangled mass of junk, and not worth salvage efforts. Besides, the pontoon was filling fast, and it wouldn't be long before the craft would be three quarters submerged and a menace to navigation in those waters. Yes, it was best to blow it up and sink it below the surface of the China Sea. Yet a plane had always been to Dave something that was almost alive, and human. It always hurt a little bit to see one of man's air creations destroyed. Yes, even when destruction was necessary.

And so as the time bomb plopped down into the cockpit Dave swallowed hard, gave the doomed plane a quick little salute of honor, and then faced the Sergeant again.

"Say, is Air Vice Marshal Bostworth at Singapore, Sergeant?" he asked. "Boy, I've got the yen to tear a mile wide strip off him when we meet. We've been floating around for over five hours. Did you know that? He said that.... What's the matter?"

Dave stopped short and asked the last because the Sergeant had suddenly stiffened and gone pale under the heavy tan on his face.

"Fancy you can speak to the Air Vice Marshal personally, sir," the Sergeant said in a hoarse whisper. "He's just behind you, waiting in the navigation compartment."

"He's *what*?" Dave gasped and felt his knees go rubbery and weak.

---

## CHAPTER FIVE
### *Official Explanations*

---

It was only the matter of a couple of seconds, but it seemed to Dave Dawson that it was a hundred years before he could dig up strength enough to turn around. When he did he saw the tall, thin faced figure of Air Vice Marshal Bostworth seated in the navigator's chair not ten feet from where he stood. The high ranking officer's eyes were slightly narrowed, and there was a glittering chill in their depths that made Dave wonder if he hadn't better just push open the Catalina's hull door and jump out to the sharks. Maybe they would be easier on him.

"Come in, you two, and shut the door!" the senior officer suddenly snapped. Then looking past the two rescued pilots, he added, "That's all, Sergeant. Tell Flight Lieutenant Baker to take off and go to maximum ceiling and cruise about until further orders. Hop to it, man!"

The Sergeant sprang into action, and so did Dave and Freddy. They stepped quickly into the navigation room and closed the door behind them. Dave gulped a couple of times and took the plunge.

"Sorry, sir, I guess I spoke out of turn," he said lamely. "It was dumb."

Air Vice Marshal Bostworth gave him a look that could cut right through steel.

"Very dumb, Flight Lieutenant, to use your native tongue!" he snapped. Then wiping the anger from his face, and grinning, he said, "But, I can't say I blame you. Would have been a bit put out, myself, if I'd been in your place. However, it was something that couldn't be helped. But sit down, sit down, you two. A spot of coffee, or tea, or rum, or something? It must have been a bit of an ordeal for you."

"Nothing for me, sir," Freddy spoke up. "I'm quite all right, sir."

"Me, too," Dave said with a nod. "But, holy.... I mean, it was certainly a surprise to learn that you were out here, sir. I thought the Harkness' captain was kidding me at first. And as for what's happened since he told us, well.... Well, we're both in a sweet flat spin."

The senior officer started to speak but checked himself as there came the faint *crump* of the exploding time bomb above the roar of the Catalina's engines as the pilot up forward took her off the water and aloft. As though by mutual agreement all three in the navigation room glanced down out of the porthole at the disc of frothy white water that marked where the Fairey Swordfish had met her end.

"Well, that's one less plane England has," Air Vice Marshal Bostworth said with a sad note in his voice.

"And I'd rather not meet up with Captain Standers for a while," Dave grunted. "Darn that submarine! It...."

He cut himself off short as the Air Vice Marshal whirled around and stared at him wide eyed.

"Submarine?" the senior officer echoed sharply. "What the devil are you talking about? Weren't you shot down by plane? A plane with R.A.F. markings? That's what I imagined."

"Plane?" Dave himself echoed. "Gosh, no! We saw some signals, and wondered what...."

"Wait a minute," the Air Vice Marshal stopped him. "Perhaps you'd better begin at the beginning, and tell me everything. Every little detail, and don't leave out a thing. Start with when Captain Standers, of the Harkness, summoned you to his quarters to give you my orders for a two hour patrol."

Dave glanced at Freddy, but the English youth shook his head.

"You tell it, Dave," he said.

Dave shrugged, stared at his two hands for a moment to get things arranged in his own mind, and then told detail for detail of their movements and actions from the time they were summoned by the commander of the Harkness, right up to when they scrambled aboard the patrol Catalina. Air Vice Marshal Bostworth listened in silence, but the frown on his face deepened as Dave talked along. And by the time the Yank born R.A.F. ace had finished his little speech there was both anger and worry glowing in the senior officer's eyes. Even when Dave finally stopped talking he didn't say a thing for several long moments. He sat puffing hard on a thin stemmed pipe he clutched between his teeth and scowled darkly at the clouds of blue smoke that curled upward.

"Damnedest thing ever!" he finally muttered. "A Jap sub, eh? Of course it was a Jap, right enough. We've suspected that they've been sneaking close into these waters whenever they got the chance. But to come to the surface and blast away at you chaps! Well.... Well, I'll be blessed if that isn't a new one. Quite sure you couldn't make head nor tail out of their heliograph signals, eh?"

"Quite, sir," Freddy said quietly.

"Not a single blink meant a thing," Dave said with a curt shake of his head. "They certainly weren't any Morse letters or numbers that I ever learned."

"A code of their own, no doubt," Air Vice Marshal Bostworth grunted. "Well, before I start my little tale let me explain why you had to float around so long. Only I and the Admiral commanding knew that I'd radioed those orders to the Harkness, you see? I had expected to be at the Air Base to meet you but I got tied up on an inspection tour of some emergency fields on the Johore side, and didn't get back until long after I expected to. It gave me a bit of a start, I can tell you, not to find you waiting, and to see the Harkness riding at anchor in the Strait. Went aboard at once and received another start when I learned you had taken off. So I hurried ashore, routed out this Catalina crew, and came hunting for you. Thank God, we got to you in time!"

"We were beginning to feel less happy by the second, sir," Dave said with an apologetic grin. "But one thing I can't figure is, why weren't there patrol planes out? Why didn't some other plane pick us up long before then? But we didn't see a single plane or surface ship during the whole time. We.... Hey! England's not at war with Japan, is she?"

"Not a declared war by either side, anyway," Air Vice Marshal Bostworth replied gravely. "However, we are watching each other like a couple of strange cats. And if you want my opinion on the matter I think the Japs are going to have a go at us inside of ten days at the most."

Dave stiffened slightly and glanced at the calendar hanging on the compartment wall. It told him that today was the sixth of December, Nineteen Hundred and Forty-One. He looked at Freddy and gave him a sly wink, and then turned to the Air Vice Marshal.

"Then that's why you came out from England in a hurry, eh?" he murmured. "The Japs are actually going to be saps, huh?"

The Air Intelligence officer smiled faintly at Dawson's remark, but shook his head and raised a cautioning finger.

"That is the spirit, Dawson," he said, "but don't be carried away by the belief that the Japs would ... would be push-overs, as they say in your country. As a matter of fact, the one mistake we have made most in this blasted war, and during the years leading up to it, too, has been to underestimate the strength and ability of the enemy. The Japs may be saps, as you say, but that won't stop them from attacking if they think they hold the winning hand. And I'm afraid they do believe they hold it."

"But they would be bashing their crazy heads against a stone wall!" Freddy Farmer protested. "I mean if they dared to have a go at Singapore. I've always been told that Singapore is every bit as impregnable as Gibraltar."

"From sea attack, yes," Air Vice Marshal Bostworth said. "But from the air? That is something else again. And as far as Singapore is concerned, the greatest weakness in its defense is not on the Island at all."

"Not on the Island, sir?" Dave Dawson echoed. "I don't think I get you."

"The water supply," the senior officer said. "It comes from Johore on the mainland side of the Strait, and is piped over the causeway. Blast Singapore's water supply and the lads on the Island would have a pretty bad time of it. However, that's neither here nor there for the moment. Dawson, you asked just a moment ago why didn't some other plane pick you up before this one. I'll tell you. Because there weren't any other planes in the air. I recalled all patrols early this morning, and grounded all planes."

The Air Vice Marshal paused for a moment, and although a thousand questions hovered on the boys' lips, they knew enough to hold their tongues.

"It's hard to tell the story," Bostworth continued presently with a frown, "because there are so many parts of it that we don't know a thing about. In a nutshell, it's this. Everything we do out here is known in detail in Berlin, Rome, and Tokio within a few hours. The blighters couldn't be better informed if we broadcast every move we make over the radio. They are finding out everything, worse luck. That was why I was sent out here. To find the leak, or leaks, and plug 'em up. As you both know, the population of Singapore is as mixed in nationalities as any other spot in the whole world. I'll wager that you could find a man from every country in the world within the limits of Singapore. Not only is it a great naval base of England's, it is also one of the great trading ports of the world. And you can be very sure that the city, itself, and the waterfront, is a thriving place for spies, right now more than ever before."

The senior officer paused for breath and stared thoughtfully out one of the portholes. The Catalina was still climbing steadily, but it had not reached an altitude where it was necessary to reach for the small portable oxygen kits fitted to the wall.

"I've been out here almost a week," the Air Intelligence officer suddenly went on, "and what little I've discovered leads me to believe that all information about our military preparations is leaving Singapore by air. No, not radio. I mean by plane. By British plane."

"A dirty rat in the R.A.F., sir?" Dave gasped as though the very thought of such a thing were a sacrilege.

"We've caught the type several times in the past," Air Vice Marshal Bostworth said grimly. "Yes, to be perfectly frank with you. I've checked and rechecked the service history of every single member of Singapore R.A.F. personnel, from the Brass Hats right down to the lowest grade aircraftsman, but a fine lot of good it's done me. I can't find a single thing that even begins to look suspicious. Yet I'm sure there are one or more Axis secret agents out here wearing the R.A.F. uniform."

The senior officer stopped to raise a silencing hand as Dave started to interrupt.

"I know that sounds crazy," he said. "I mean, that the spy is in the R.A.F. out here. But here is my reason for thinking so. Rather, my reasons for thinking so. I've made a few tests. I've let certain bits of information become known, and then used a secret gadget we've perfected that can pick up any kind of radio broadcast on any wave-length within a radius of two hundred miles. And can do it while nearby powerful stations are operating. But we didn't hear a single broadcast of which we didn't know the code and couldn't decipher easily. I've checked all ship movements, and all movements of troops going over the causeway. And all civilians, too. However, all the information I had purposely let slip reached the Berlin Government in a very short time. That was reported to me by my own agents. So I was sure all of the information left here by plane. It must have.

But.... But I must confess I didn't even dream they did it the way your experience seems to prove they do it."

"Then that two hour patrol we were supposed to have made, and did make?" Dave said with a puzzled frown. "You expected us to spot the spy in his plane tearing off to pass on the information to somebody else? But maybe we might not have given him a single glance. At least, not a second glance."

Air Vice Marshal Bostworth shook his head and struck a match to fire up his dead pipe.

"No, not exactly that," he said presently. "I let out a rather valuable bit of information concerning coming reenforcements out here, and then grounded all planes. Used the excuse of general overhaul and inspection. At the same time I arranged for you chaps to buzz around over the Strait. First, I wanted to see if our little spy friend would risk it to fly off with his bit of information in the face of my grounding order. If he did, we could jolly well radio you chaps his direction and orders to head him off at all cost. Secondly, if the blighter didn't try to sneak off ... which he didn't, blast him ... I wanted you chaps out there to spot any plane of *any* type that might attempt to contact you in the air. In other words I was counting on you chaps to help me get a line on the *other* plane that I believed was flying out each day from Japanese controlled Indo-China to contact their man in our forces. I was hoping for a description of the plane, what direction it came from, and so forth. I had thought up a little stunt to pull.... But that's out, now. Our friend isn't contacting another plane. He is, of course, contacting a submarine. A Jap sub, no doubt, but I'll wager a thousand pounds it's commanded by a trained Nazi. So you see, when you didn't show up, and I found you floating on the water, I thought that you'd had a bit of a go with this supposedly other plane, and come off second best. Good lord, though, that submarine was bold as brass to surface and actually blaze away at you! To me that means they're getting very cocky. And of course I'm speaking of the Jap johnnies."

"Contacts a Jap tin can, huh, and probably drops his information by signal buoy?" Dave murmured more to himself. "The sub slips on to sea and radioes the stuff to its nearest base."

"Correct," Air Vice Marshal Bostworth said with a curt nod. "And from that particular base it is relayed on to Tokio. And from Tokio it goes to Berlin. And Hitler knows all about the very latest things we've accomplished out here. And Tokio has another bit of information on what she'll be up against when she attacks us."

"And she will, you feel sure, sir?" Freddy Farmer spoke for the first time in many minutes.

"Unfortunately, there isn't the slightest doubt of it," the Air Intelligence officer replied. "Yes, we expect war, rather, we expect an attack, and very soon. We're getting ready for it just as fast as we can. However, our forces are not strong, particularly in the air, and what we've got to find out ... and it'll probably require a miracle to find it out ... is just where, when, and how the Japs plan to strike. I don't think it will be by sea. And I don't think it will be by land down the Malay Peninsula *unless* they are forced to. I have a feeling they will attempt a quick knockout by air. That perhaps they'll have a go at Hongkong and Singapore at the same time. I don't know. If only I could catch the sly beggar who's getting out all the information, I could put a plan to work that might get very good results that will tip the Japs' hand as to just what they will try once they get the go-ahead word from Berlin. But...."

The Air Vice Marshal sighed heavily and gave an angry shake of his head.

"But so long as the leak remains," he grated through clenched teeth, "we're definitely in the soup. And heaven only knows what may come of it. We haven't the fighting strength we need to beat off an all out attack. And I'm very much afraid we're not going to get reenforcements in time."

The Air Vice Marshal fell silent for a few moments, stared unseeing off into space, and absently tapped the stem of his pipe against his strong teeth. Eventually he grunted as though he had reached some kind of a decision, and switched his gaze to the two R.A.F. youths.

"We've got to find out what the Japs, coached by the Nazis of course, are planning," he said slowly. "I think there's a way we can do it. True, it's about one chance in a thousand of succeeding. And.... Well, the attempt could well possibly cost the lives of a couple of brave chaps."

The Intelligence Officer emphasized the last with a faint gesture of his hand, and for the next minute or so there was no sound in the navigation compartment save the muffled roar of the engines outside. Dave looked at Freddy, caught his grim nod, and turned to the Air Vice Marshal.

"Well, I know a couple of fellows who would like to take a crack at it, sir," he said in a quiet, steady voice.

# CHAPTER SIX
## *The Devil's Den*

The Air Ministry official looked at them, smiled and seemed to let clamped air out of his lungs.

"I knew, of course, that you'd say that," he said. "But I was not exaggerating when I said you might pay for your efforts with your lives. Strictly speaking, it is not an Air Force job. I mean, there may or may not be any flying attached to it. The task is very definitely Intelligence work. Lord knows any one of us Intelligence chaps out here in the Far East would be only too glad to have a go at it. However, every British Intelligence Johnnie in these parts is well known to Axis agents here. Just as we have a pretty good idea who is working against us ... though we haven't yet laid them all by the heels."

The Air Vice Marshal paused and gave an angry shake of his head as though he were getting himself all mixed up.

"I'd better tell what little I know," he said, "and perhaps between us we can fill some of the holes with close guesses. Well, here goes. In the city of Singapore, near the waterfront, there is a street called Bukum Street. It is actually little more than an alley crowded on both sides with rickety two story frame buildings with open store fronts on the lower floors. They say that when you want to find Bukum Street you don't bother to ask a native policeman. You simply stand still and sniff. Then follow the most terrible smell of them all, and at its source you will find Bukum Street.

"Halfway along the waterfront side of Bukum Street there is a little spice and coffee shop very appropriately called the Devil's Den. It is owned and operated by a man named Serrangi who looks as old as the city itself. He is a Sumatran, as far as we can find out, but I fancy he has a little of all the bloods of the Far East in his veins. He is a hideous looking creature. Face terribly scarred, and he has a cast in his right eye. But he is more diabolically clever than Satan, himself. We know that he is a thief, that he would murder any one for you for the price of a few pennies, and, that there is no intrigue brewing in which he hasn't got at least the tip of his finger. But, to our discredit, if you wish, the British Singapore authorities haven't been able to catch him redhanded in a single thing. Personally, I think we should throw the beggar in prison, and be done with it. Unfortunately, though, the white man's laws do not operate that way. Also, Serrangi has a tremendous influence with the native population. To punish Serrangi without proof of guilt might stir up a beautiful native riot. And so, we've only been able to watch and wait ... and hope. And to date we're no better off than we were two years ago."

"Serrangi and his Devil's Den is the leak, sir?" murmured Freddy Farmer as the senior officer paused for breath.

"We don't know," was the blunt reply. "You see, this business is so confoundedly twisted up that anything might be possible. It might even be possible that Serrangi is loyal to the Crown, though I'm sure I would drop dead from the shock if such proof even came to my attention. But I'm only telling you what we suspect, not what we know. And the first item on our long list of suspicions is that all Axis spies entering or leaving Singapore do so through the Devil's Den. In short that Serrangi's place is ... you might say ... the clearing house for information. A couple of months ago a known Nazi spy ... one high up in the Gestapo by the way ... was picked up as he left the Devil's Den. We found nothing of interest on his person, however. And we could not prove that he had gone to Serrangi's for any other reason than to make a few purchases. Also, not over two weeks ago one of our agents was last seen entering Serrangi's. We never saw him again. We haven't even found his body yet. And an authorized search of the Devil's Den brought to light absolutely nothing!"

The Air Vice Marshal paused and clenched both fists in a helpless gesture.

"Working in the East is so utterly different from working in the West!" he said bitterly. "In England we could close up a place like the Devil's Den, and burn it to the ground, if we thought it was necessary. And toss the lot of them in prison, to boot. But you can't do that sort of thing out here. Not unless you want to have native trouble on your hands. Anyway, we feel certain that if we could learn even a few of the secrets of Serrangi's place we would be able to profit as much as though we had an extra dozen divisions of trained troops, together with aircraft, and the like. Now, here is the part that concerns you. And...."

The Intelligence Officer stopped talking abruptly and stared hard at the two youths.

"This is entirely outside your line of duty," he said almost harshly. "Just because I am telling you all this does not mean in the slightest that you must agree to go through with the thing. You two are R.A.F. pilots, and there's still plenty for you to do as such. I mean.... Well, that is...."

"Why not just tell us, sir?" Dave interrupted with an encouraging grin as the senior officer fumbled for words. "If we get cold feet, or think we'd flop the thing, we promise to tell you."

"Thanks, Dawson," the Air Vice Marshal said gravely. "Very well, then. I want to get you two into Serrangi's place, by hook or by crook. No one knows you have come to Singapore. I mean, the Harkness has arrived but you weren't aboard. Of course, by now those damn Axis agents, that have been virtually living in my pockets without my knowing it, must know that two pilots took off from the Harkness before she reached port; that their arrival at Singapore is long over-due, and that this Catalina has gone out to try and find them. Well, this Catalina is going to return to Singapore R.A.F. Base, her flight a failure. Yes, we found the half submerged wreckage of the Harkness' plane. But, *no* sign of the two who were in it. Examination of the wreckage showed that the craft had obviously been shot down. How, we don't know. We are only certain that the two pilots in her are dead. The sharks must have got them."

Dave Dawson licked his lower lip and glanced sidewise at Freddy Farmer.

"Imagine how the shark that got you feels!" he chuckled.

"Is that so!" the English youth snapped. "Well, it's always been difficult to tell from the look on your face whether you were dead or alive. So you fit the part perfectly, my lad."

"Ouch!" Dave cried and winced. Then grinning at the Intelligence officer he said, "Go ahead, sir. Don't mind us. It's the way we let off steam, I guess."

"More should adopt the method," the Air Vice Marshal said firmly. "But this business is far from a joke. It is far more serious than I can tell you. To be very brutal about it, by this time tomorrow it's quite possible that you and Farmer*may be*...."

The senior officer didn't finish. Instead he stuck out a clenched fist and then extended the thumb downward toward the compartment floor. The gesture was more explanatory than words. Dave felt a tingling chill ripple through his heart but he kept the grin on his face. After a moment the Air Intelligence officer continued.

"You two will be reported as definitely dead," he said. "I'll make no bones about being certain of that. I fancy we'll even drink a silent toast to you at evening mess. You know, do the thing up right for the benefit of listening ears or watching eyes. Meantime, you two will proceed to Bukum Street and go into the Devil's Den. Both of you speak German, and French, and, of course, English. You will have to decide for yourselves what language you want to use. You'll be.... Well, you'll be wharf rats to all appearances. Or you can be a couple of French merchant sailors stranded in Singapore after jumping ship. You can be a couple of Germans rescued from a China boat sunk off shore. Fact is, you can be anything you like. It will be frankly up to you to decide each move as you go along."

"Aren't you just a bit ahead of things, sir?" Freddy Farmer said as the flush mounted in his cheeks. "I mean, how do we get ashore from this Catalina? And what about clothes?"

"That's the easiest part of the whole thing," the other replied. "We'll talk about that later. Now, the moment you enter the Devil's Den your lives will be in your own hands. I cannot tell you what you will find. I cannot tell you what will happen. I'd be a blasted miracle maker, if I could. But, I can tell you this. We know the identification code word of Nazi agents out here in the Far East. It's three words, as a matter of fact. *Der Fuehrer's Tag.* Meaning, of course, The Leader's Day. How and when you use it, I do not know. And...."

The Air Vice Marshal paused and groaned softly.

"And I have got to tell you this," he said presently. "The British Intelligence agent who entered the Devil's Den two weeks ago, never to be seen again, was *also* armed with the code word, or words. I am as certain, though, as I am that I'm sitting here, that the Nazi agent identification signal has not been changed. They still use it, and you two will have to decide the proper time, and place, to mention it."

"A salute when you take a sip of your coffee might be a good idea," Dave said, looking at Freddy. "Sort of say it under your breath, but loud enough for anyone sitting close to hear."

Dave turned his head and looked at Air Vice Marshal Bostworth.

"Your plan is for us to be a couple of Axis agents reporting, isn't it, Sir?" he asked.

The Air Intelligence officer gave Dawson a look of frank admiration, and nodded instantly.

"Exactly that," he said. "I'm sure new agents sent out go straight to Serrangi's place. Of course, there may be some one to whom they report. I don't know. That's the risk you've got to take. But here's a plan to cover that part. You can be a couple of Axis agents shipping from China to ... say Australia. Your boat was sunk.... I can give you the names of several ships sunk in the South China Sea recently ... and you were put ashore in Singapore. You, of course, have known of the Devil's Den, and you know the code words for identification."

"That's a splendid arrangement, sir!" Freddy Farmer spoke up excitedly. "That way we won't have to show any papers. We can say we lost everything at sea. But...."

The English youth stopped short and scowled.

"But what, Farmer?" Air Vice Marshal Bostworth prompted.

It was a few seconds before Freddy acted as though he had heard.

"I was thinking, sir," he said slowly, "what if nobody pays any attention to us? What if we just go into this Devil's Den, and nothing happens?"

"We've got to hope hard that something will," the Air Intelligence officer said grimly. "And I don't think you need worry about nobody paying any attention to you. You'll be strangers, and you'll look the part of seamen put ashore from a lost ship. I'm quite certain that Serrangi keeps a very close watch on everybody who comes into his place. However, that's the blasted sticker about this thing. It's no more and no less than a blind stab in the dark. It may gain us nothing, and then again, it may gain us a lot. And ... it may get you both a knife in your back before you've been in the place five minutes. I pray to God not, but that's the chance you'll be taking. To sum it up bluntly, you'll simply be grabbing at possible straws, and...."

"And there may not be any to grab," Dave grunted as the other hesitated.

"Precisely!" the senior officer said and made a wry face. "You'll be taking a wild, blind shot in the dark to connect with something that will lead you to the top rankers in the Axis espionage system working in Singapore."

"It would certainly be a break if the spy you're gunning for at Singapore R.A.F. Base uses Serrangi's as a contact place," Dave said. "I think I could spot an R.A.F. lad with my eyes shut."

"Not this one, I fancy," the Air Vice Marshal said. "He may be R.A.F. on the surface when he's on duty, but the blighter is Nazi at heart. He'll be clever, and twice as cruel, too. But, if you should be lucky enough to contact him ... rather, spot him ... a lot of my worries would be over. Once I find out that beggar's identity I've got a very neat little plan already to be put into operation. That, however, would be like asking for a miracle on a silver platter."

"But, supposing we do tag him," Dave persisted. "How do you plan for us to get word to you, sir?"

"I've arranged for that," the senior officer said. "In front of the Raffles Hotel, which is perhaps the easiest thing to find in all Singapore, there's always a gathering of peddlers and hawkers who will sell anything to soldiers and civilians alike. In peace times they made quite a good thing out of it from the tourist trade, but they are not doing so well now that half the world is at war. However they still cluster about in front of the Raffles hoping to make a few pennies. Anyway, one of them is a horrible looking creature. He is not more than five feet tall, and bent over at that. He wears a dirty white patch over his right eye, and the thumb on the left hand is missing. He is always there, and you couldn't possibly miss him. Put any message you have for me in Air Intelligence Code Six-X-Seven, walk past the man with the patch over his right eye, and toss the wadded message into the gutter, as though it were a bit of paper you were throwing away. And.... By the by, you know the Air Intelligence Code Six-X-Seven, of course?"

"Yes, sir," Freddy spoke for both of them. "By heart, sir."

"Good," Air Vice Marshal Bostworth said and gave them a pleased nod. "Well, do as I say, if you have any message you want transmitted to me. However, be sure and just walk by the beggar, and toss the bit of paper into the gutter. Do not turn to him or look at him. And for heaven's sake don't speak to him. You'll probably lose the man his life if you speak to him. And I hasten to tell you that he is one of the best British counter espionage agents in Singapore. Well, so much for that. Now, any other questions?"

Dave looked at Freddy Farmer and nodded.

"Go ahead with that question you asked awhile back," he said. "I guess that's the important one, now."

The English youth looked blank for a moment, then his face brightened as he realized what Dave was talking about.

"Oh, yes, quite," he said and turned to Air Vice Marshal Bostworth. "It's that question I asked about getting ashore from this Catalina, and clothes, sir."

"Simple, quite simple," the senior officer replied with a faint wave of his hand. "I only hope the rest of this blasted business will be equally as simple. Well...."

The man paused, looked at his watch, and then glanced out the porthole at the blood red sun that was balancing like a ball on the western horizon line. Its flaming red rays fanned out across the sky to bathe everything in a pinkish glow. Even the wings of the Catalina were touched by the glow that bounced off their glossy surfaces and seeped in through the ports to the interior of the compartment. The dying sun was a beautiful, breath catching sight ... but not right at the moment for Dave Dawson and Freddy Farmer. Their thoughts were not on beautiful things, now, but on many other things, not the least of which was possible death by tomorrow's setting sun.

"Well, in an hour it will be darkish, sort of," the Air Vice Marshal continued speaking. "When it is we're going to head back toward Singapore. I will have the radio operator send word that our search failed, and that I'm having this flyingboat land in Keppel Harbor as I wish to go direct to the Government buildings in the city. We will land in the harbor and the crew will break out two of the collapsible boats we carry aboard. I will go ashore in one. You two will use the other. Under cover of darkness you can easily reach some section of Singapore's waterfront undetected. Simply go ashore and release the air valve in your boat. It will fill up and sink at once. As for clothes...."

The senior officer paused and smiled faintly.

"This is not the first time I have used this Catalina for Intelligence work," he said. "In fact, it is used almost exclusively for such jobs. You'd be surprised the stuff we have aboard this craft. We carry all kinds of clothes, from a German soldier's uniform on up to almost anything you could mention. Don't worry, before you leave this Catalina you'll look so much like a couple of rescued sailors from a China to Australia boat your own families wouldn't recognize you. Later I'll give you facts of an actual sinking to make your story ring true. Now, what else, eh?"

Dave started to speak, but thought better of it after an instant's hesitation, and closed his mouth. Air Vice Marshal Bostworth gave him a sharp quizzical glance.

"Yes, Dawson?" he encouraged. "What is it? Ask anything you like. After all, this is not going to be any tea party that you two are setting out on. If you've got something to ask me, go right ahead. Later on, you might regret not having asked it."

Dave hesitated a couple of more seconds, then shrugged.

"Well, maybe it's a crazy question, sir," he said slowly, "but somehow I always like to be on the safe side. I mean, I like to be sure about a couple of things in advance, when I stick my neck out, if you get what I mean?"

"I think I understand, a little," the other said. "But perhaps you'd better make yourself a bit clearer, eh?"

The American born R.A.F. ace took a deep breath as though he were about to dive off into icy waters. Then he blurted it out.

"The crew of this Catalina, sir," he said. "You admit that there is some Nazi agent at the Singapore R.A.F. Base. A lad you haven't been able to lay by the heels yet. Well, what I mean is this. Those aboard this flyingboat know who we are. The sergeant gunner asked us if we were Dawson and Farmer when we came aboard. Well.... That is to say.... I mean...."

Dave stumbled to a halt and flushed a deep red.

"You mean, how about the loyalty of the crew of this Catalina?" the Air Vice Marshal helped him out.

"Yes, sir," Dave said with a nod.

"A perfectly fair question," the other replied. "I'll describe their loyalty in this way, then. *I* would reveal your true identity to the Nazi agents in Singapore before any one of them would."

"That's all I want to know," Dave said. "Fair enough. Any better wouldn't do. How about you, Freddy?"

"Quite," the English youth said. "Oh, very definitely and absolutely!"

"Then what are we waiting for?" Dave said, turning back to Air Vice Marshal Bostworth with a grin. "Let's get going and not keep old Serrangi waiting any longer than we have to!"

## CHAPTER SEVEN
### *The Jaws of Death*

Night had come again to Singapore. From one end of the Island to the other all was cloaked in velvety darkness save where light made by man thrust aside the shadows. At Raffles Hotel they still danced, and at the famous city cafes they still drank and watched worn out floor shows, even though the nearness of war in the Far East seemed to hang in the very air like a shroud. Even in the poorer sections, and in the slums, there were sounds of merry-making. It was almost as though rich man and beggar alike were enjoying themselves as much as they could before the sword of Mars came slashing down on that section of the earth.

In the unspeakably smelly alley that is known as Bukum Street two figures slouched along as though they didn't have an idea in the world where they were going, and cared even less when they got there. At every little opened front shop they paused and gaped vacant eyed at the collection of wares on display. Sometimes they muttered things to each other in low tones. Sometimes they said nothing, and just stared. And more times than not the storekeepers instantly sized them up as very poor prospects for a sale and waved them on their way.

Presently they both halted in their tracks as though by unspoken signal and stared half a block ahead at a two story wooden building on the other side of the street. It was much the same as all the others save there was no shop on the lower floor of this building, and therefore it had no open front. On the contrary, it had a front door and windows, and hanging from a bracket that protruded from the door was a sign with somebody's idea of His Satanic Majesty painted on it in red.

"That's us, Freddy!" muttered the taller of the pair. "A crummy looking joint, isn't it?"

"Much worse!" came the half muffled reply. "And good Lord, this awful smell does come from there! So blasted thick and heavy, I can almost see it coming out the front door."

"Yeah," Dave Dawson murmured. "And if it's from the brand of coffee they serve in there I'm afraid I'm going to be an awful flop before I even get started. I couldn't keep anything down that smells like that for longer than one millionth of one split second. Holy catfish! Do you suppose this Serrangi runs a slaughter house on the side? Boy! That stench almost bounces when it hits you."

"That's right," Freddy Farmer agreed. "We should have remembered to bring clothespins. Well, worse luck for us, we didn't. But what do you say, Dave? Shall we get on with it?"

"Why not, we've come this far," Dave grunted, and started slouching forward again. "But, look, Freddy."

"At what?"

"No, I mean, listen!" Dave hissed out the corner of his mouth. "Bostworth handed us a pip this time. Like trying to win a ball game in the last of the ninth with your team a couple of hundred runs behind. What I mean is, that anything can happen from here on. Just like Bostworth said, when we go through that door we're on our own. We may strike out on three pitched balls, and then again we may run into something mighty valuable to him. But there's two guys we've got to look out for all the time. You and me. Now, if by any chance things do get rough, keep close to me. We make it or don't, together. Okay?"

"Absolutely," Freddy Farmer replied quietly. "Shoulder to shoulder all the time, Dave, of course."

"Maybe in Serrangi's place we'd better make it back to back," Dave said. "They're experts with knives in this part of the world, so I've been told. So if we get back to back when things break bad, we'll at least see who's doing what."

"I'd feel happier if we were armed," Freddy Farmer said. "I suppose Bostworth was right when he said that carrying arms might get us into trouble if we were searched. Just the same, though, I'd feel a lot happier if we were armed."

"You and me each, brother!" Dave breathed softly as they neared the front door of the smelly place. "You and me each! However, maybe we'll live to bless him for that word of caution."

"Just so's we live will please me enough!" Freddy muttered. Then as they came almost abreast of the door, he added softly, "I think it would be best to speak bad French in this place. Much better than English or German, don't you think?"

"Check, it'll be French," Dave said and gave Freddy's arm a quick squeeze. "Well, luck to us both. And do I hope I can keep that coffee down! Okay, follow me, my little man."

Dave hesitated a moment, took a deep breath, and then pushed in through the front door of the Devil's Den. He was instantly smacked in the face by a babble of sound, and a stench that almost made his nose drop off. For a second he could see only blurred yellow shadows, the place was so heavy with cheap cigarette, and water-pipe smoke. Then as he spotted an empty table to his left he gave a jerk of his head to Freddy, and shuffled across the filthy floor and sat down. Leaning back he lazily surveyed the place with his eyes. He had seen an awful lot of terrible places since the first day of war, but the Devil's Den topped them all, and then some. It was half store and half coffee shop. Along one wall of the room, that was some forty feet deep and three quarters as wide, was a series of shelves filled with bins that contained everything from spices, tea, and native coffee to pith helmets and old army uniforms. On the opposite side was a row of battered tables so badly stained it was impossible to tell the original color of the wood. The sirupy coffee of the hot countries was spilled all over the table, and it was quite probable that no efforts had been made to mop up the sticky drippings in the last six months. And where there wasn't coffee there was dirt or cigarette ash.

Seated at the tables was a mixture of all races from Suez to Saigon, and from Hongkong to Borneo. There were Malays and Chinese, Sumatrans and Tamils from India, Filipinos and Punjabis, Arabs and Siamese, Persians, and a smattering that had once claimed kinship with the white races but had sunk so low they were no longer any part of a white man.

Dave's heart looped over and his stomach churned as he let his sleepy, seemingly uninterested gaze travel slowly about the room. Many of those there looked at him in return, but only for the smallest part of a second. It seemed to be sort of an unwritten law that you didn't stare too hard or too long at your fellow coffee drinkers in the Devil's Den. Some of them didn't so much as lift their heads when Dave and Freddy entered. Either they weren't interested in newcomers or else they were too full of the poison of the Far East to get up the strength.

There was one, however, who took real interest in the arrival of the two slouching ones in dirty sea water stained clothes. He was standing near the steaming coffee urns at the far end of the room near a door. As Dave's eyes passed over the scarred face with the cast in the right eye it was all the young American could do to check himself from starting violently. Serrangi's face would certainly scare even Satan, himself. The man was not very tall, and he seemed not to have much flesh on his bones. Yet somehow he gave you the impression of coiled steel springs ready to lash out in any and all directions. A scarecrow, perhaps, but with the strength of a killer in his thin arms, legs, and body. But it was the eyes. Particularly the one with the cast. That one was a dirty grey white; a dirty grey white beam of light that seemed to go right through you and read your innermost thoughts on the way. For perhaps a split second Dave had a look at the mysterious Serrangi, but in that brief period of time he saw all he ever wanted to see of the man.

He let his lazy gaze travel on and then brought it to rest on an evil faced native waiter sliding toward them. The man came to a halt at Dave's elbow and hissed something in a tongue Dave couldn't catch.

"Bring coffee," Dave growled in heavily accented French. Then as an afterthought, "And cigarettes, too!"

"So?" the native snarled right back in the same tongue. "Here one sees the color of a man's money first."

Dave glared and reluctantly pulled a small silver coin from his pocket and slapped it on the table.

"The color of a silver knife, eh?" he grunted and jerked his head toward the urns. "Go bring us some!"

The native waiter half bowed, flicked out a grimy paw and the silver coin wasn't there anymore. At the same time he slithered around and glided away. Dave had the feeling as though a snake had just wiggled across his chest, and it was all he could do to stop the shiver that welled up inside of him. Instead he slumped over the table and rubbed a hand tentatively up and down the side of his face. He did it to cover up the movement of his lips as he whispered to Freddy.

"Nice joint!" he breathed. "I wonder if the floorshow's as good. Gives you the creeps, doesn't it?"

"Goose pimples all over!" Freddy replied. "Am jolly well sure they'll be permanent. Notice how our little friend gave us the eye? And is still doing it? Rotten looking chap, for fair. Should jail him because of his face alone. Horrible fellow. He.... Heads up, Dave!"

The last just barely carried to Dave's ears but there was a tremor in Freddy's voice that was just as good as a wild yell of alarm. He cut short what he might have said to the English youth, made a final pass at the side of his face then cupped his chin in his hand and stared moodily off into space. Every part of him, though, was on the alert, and in less than no time he realized why Freddy Farmer had breathed the warning. A filthy native who had been seated by the front door when they entered was slowly edging toward the table next to theirs, but not noticeably so, unless you were on your guard, which good old Freddy Farmer was proving he was!

Still staring off into space Dave watched the native out of the corner of his eye. The man finally reached the table, muttered what sounded like an apology to two half cast Malays seated at the table, slid into a chair and promptly to all intent and purposes rested his forehead on his folded arms on the table and went sound asleep. Even the sound of his breathing was like that of a half doped man, but Dave Dawson was not fooled one single bit. And neither was Freddy Farmer. One of the dirty native's ears showed and they both felt certain that every sound they made was being registered by that ear.

Shifting his position to a more comfortable one Dave let his eyes meet Freddy's for the fraction of a second. In that swift period of time a world of understanding passed between them. That native who faked sleeping off the effects of some drug at the next table was unquestionably one of Serrangi's men. He was there to eavesdrop on their talk. To listen to every word they said, and perhaps send a signal to Serrangi that could well be their death warrant. However, that thought cheered them rather than caused icy fingers to clutch at their hearts. If the man *was* one of Serrangi's spies he was playing right into their hands. What better opportunity could they ask for than this one to give the code signal revealing them as Nazi agents in Singapore?

It was perfect. It was made to order. Yet, on the other hand, it seemed so perfect that Dave caught his brain swaying way over the other way. To the side of extra, extra caution. Was this in reality a trap? Would it be wise to mention the code word when a total stranger was sitting so close? Had Bostworth's agent made that mistake when he entered the Devil's Den, and it had proved to be a fatal one? Would it not be better to wait, to spend a while over their first cup of coffee before trying to contact possible Nazi agents in the room? It was perhaps best to....

Dave cut off the rest of the thought as the shadow of the filthy native waiter suddenly appeared at his elbow as though by magic. Two dirty cracked cups the size of thumb thimbles were placed in front of him and Freddy. In the cups was a smudgy brown liquid that no white man would even use to paint the side of a cow-barn. An acrid stench drifted up from each cup. It made Dave think of burning sulphur and kerosene, only not so sweet smelling. As a matter of fact, for one crazy instant he wondered if it was some deadly chemical that was going to explode in his face in the next second and blind him. He killed off that thought, however, and whipped out his hand to grab the native's arm as the man started to glide away.

"The cigarettes!" he growled. "I gave you enough to feed your filthy family for years. Bring us the cigarettes!"

The native waiter's eyes glowed up for a moment in a look of deadly hatred. But his gaze soon fell before Dave's steely one. He bobbed his head, mumbled something, and hurried away. Dave turned back to the table and picked up his cup and looked at Freddy Farmer. Suddenly he was convinced that it was do or die now, or never. He held the cup native style between his two hands, and leaned forward toward Freddy Farmer and opened his mouth to speak. But what he was about to say died in his throat. It died because in that same instant the front door of the Devil's Den was suddenly slammed open and two Singapore policemen came bursting into the room.

"*Brenti!*" one of them screamed.

It was the Malay word for "Halt!" and every man in the room, including Serrangi, himself, froze stiff in whatever position he happened to be.

## CHAPTER EIGHT
### *The Secret Message*

Like a pair of killers who would love nothing better than to blast away in all directions with the police pistols they clutched, the two Singapore policemen stood straddle legged, their black eyes seeming to focus on every face at the same time. The Devil's Den was suddenly filled with pin-dropping silence. It was more the silence of sudden death. Dave's heart slammed like a trip-hammer against his ribs, and he was sure that the sound carried throughout the room like a booming drum.

Here was something that Air Vice Marshal Bostworth hadn't so much as mentioned as a bare possibility. A raid on Serrangi's place by the native police. Supposing they were all dragged in? What would he and Freddy do? How would they be able to get out of the clutches of the local law? True, they could establish their true identities in short order. Sure, and probably be released with a thousand heart felt apologies! But a fine lot of good that would do them! Their opportunity would then be gone forever. Be gone because there were certain to be listening ears at police headquarters. Ears that would hear what they said. And a tongue or two that would take a warning back to Serrangi's. No, if they left the Devil's Den with the native police for questioning they would never enter Serrangi's again. They both would be dead before they could get both feet inside.

Yet the alternative was just as bad. Perhaps worse. If they posed as coming from a torpedoed boat headed for Australia their stories would be checked within the hour by police officials ... and be found as full of holes as a rusted sieve. As a result they would be thrown into a jail cell in nothing flat, and be kept there until they rotted before they could convince their jailers of the truth. Yes, it was something that Air Vice Marshal Bostworth hadn't even dreamed of, to say nothing of themselves. A choice of two things ... and both evil and spelling bad luck, or worse.

And so Dave's heart pounded even more furiously against his ribs as the two policemen seemed to focus their attention on Freddy and him. Was this the moment? Was this the end of something that had hardly had a beginning? Those questions and others burned through Dave's brain like liquid fire. He wanted to look at Freddy to see how his pal was taking it, but he didn't dare take his eyes off the two policemen.

Then suddenly the pair started walking slowly down the length of the room. Whenever they came to a man who was dead to the world, and had not lifted his head at their arrival, one of them would grab him by the hair, jerk up his head and glare at the man's face. One swift scrutinizing stare and then the man's head would flop down on his folded arms again, or sag chin down on his chest and roll from side to side like a toy balloon in a gentle breeze.

Eventually the two Singapore policemen came abreast of Dawson's table. For one horrible moment he lived and died a thousand times over. Then the policemen passed on to the next table to the rear. In time they reached Serrangi standing by the coffee urns. Dave heard the soft sound as the pair spoke, and the harsh nerve-grating replies from Serrangi's lips. But he didn't understand the tongue. And then, finally, when Dave's nerves were almost ready to fly apart in all directions, the two policemen wheeled about, stalked back to the front door and disappeared.

Dave held his breath waiting for the babble of sound to come from the many tongues in the place. But he was doomed to disappointment if he expected the coffee shop customers to show any excitement over the visit. They simply relaxed in their chairs, shrugged slightly at their next table neighbors, and continued on doing whatever it was they had been doing when the policemen burst into the room.

To cover his own almost overwhelming sense of relief Dave slumped over the table edge and cupped his chin in both hands and stared down at the still untouched cup of smudgey brown coffee. It was then he suddenly realized that the dirty native was no longer seated at the adjoining table. The man had disappeared as though by magic. Dave blinked at the empty chair and then quickly lowered his eyes.

"Our pal has scrammed," he breathed just loud enough for Freddy to hear. "Did he go through the floor or just evaporate in the smokey air?"

"Neither," came the hushed reply. "He slid along in back of the two bobbies. Talking with Serrangi, now. Steady! Here he comes back again."

"Don't ever miss a trick, do you!" Dave murmured and reached for his coffee cup. "Well, I'm going to pull the code words this time. I'll go plain bats if this suspense keeps up much longer. Luck to us, pal."

"And we'll probably need it, Dave. Right-o. Fire away!"

Dave waited until the shadow of the passing native fell directly across the table. Then he started the coffee cup to his lips and looked at Freddy.

"*Der Fuehrer's Tag!*" he grunted and put his lips to the vile smelling cup.

"*Ja, ja!*" Freddy Farmer grunted in reply. "*Der Fuehrer's Tag.* It cannot come soon enough to please me!"

Both spoke in pure German, and both held their breath as the shadow of the passing native seemed to linger a second on the table. Then it passed on by, and it was all either of them could do to refrain from turning around and staring directly at the man. With an effort though, they remained seated as they were. And with a thousand times greater effort they forced themselves to sip a little of the most horrible liquid they had ever tasted in their lives. It took every ounce of Dave's will power not to spit it out. Instead, though, he forced it down and had the sensation of a couple of red hot coals dropping clear down to the pit of his stomach. He waited a full minute before he dared to speak.

"Are you still alive, Freddy?" he whispered. "I'm not sure just how I feel."

"I think, so," the English youth whispered back. "At any rate, I can still talk, and see and hear. But I think we'd better not talk much, Dave. Serrangi is taking interest in us again. It's possible that he might be a lip reader."

"Or has eyes in the back of his head like you seem to have," Dave murmured. "How you can look two ways at the same time, I'll never be able to.... What's up?"

Dave cut himself off and asked the last as he saw Freddy's hand resting on the table suddenly stiffen. The English youth didn't reply for a moment. Then he spoke loudly in bad French.

"Those cigarettes!" he exclaimed. "Do we get them, or must we go someplace where they don't steal a poor man's money?"

As the English youth spoke he glared at the native waiter who was busy about something over on the other side of the room. Then as he slouched back in his chair again he flashed Dave a warning look.

"Serrangi just nodded to somebody in back of us!" he breathed behind a hand that pawed at his mouth. "To some one in back of us! Our little friend, of course. I wonder what it means?"

"I wouldn't know," Dave grunted. "But I sure am hoping like blazes. For the best, I mean. Oh-oh!"

The native had suddenly appeared at Dave's elbow. But the man didn't stop. He glided on by toward the rear of the room. As he passed, though, Dave caught the quick motion of one hand, and saw the tiny pellet pop from the man's fingers, and roll across the table to come to a stop not three inches from Dave's cup of coffee. Freddy saw it, too, and sucked in his breath in a soft hiss of excitement. Dave didn't look at him, or at the little pellet resting on the table. Instead he stared unconcernedly at the front door, and absently dropped one hand down over the pellet.

For a couple of minutes he seemingly took no interest at all in anything, but as a matter of fact his heart was thumping, and the pellet, which was a wadded up bit of paper, seemed to burn like a hot coal under his hand. At the end of two minutes, which passed like an eternity of taunting suspense, Dave drew his hand off the table, and brought the little pellet of paper along with it. Another couple of seconds and he had both hands in his lap, shielded from all eyes by the edge of the table, and was feverishly smoothing out the wadded paper with his fingers. He knew that Freddy Farmer was watching him out the corner of his eye every instant of the time, but to all appearances the English youth was taking a cat nap.

Finally Dave had the paper smoothed out. He didn't glance down at it right away, though. It was as though he were almost afraid to read whatever was written on the paper. It was as though he would read there his death warrant, or something. As a matter of fact, a million wild, crazy thoughts surged through his brain, and he could feel the little beads of cold sweat that broke out on his forehead. With an effort he shrugged the maddening thoughts aside, took a deep breath and glanced down at the paper in his hands. The scrawl was in French, and almost impossible to read. Dave had to study it hard for a few seconds before he could make out the words. When he finally did read the message his heart did nip-ups in his chest. The message was short and right to the point.

It read,

*In five minutes' walk through rear door.*

The message was unsigned. Just those seven words, but at the moment they constituted the most exciting seven words Dave Dawson had ever read in his life. He swallowed hard as a means of pushing his looping heart back down into place. Then he leaned one elbow on the table, and reached out under the table with the other hand that held the message.

"A little love note," he murmured to Freddy. "Take a look. We're getting action, pal ... maybe!"

Three minutes later Freddy Farmer had the message in his hands and had read it. His face didn't change a hair save for a tiny white spot that appeared in each cheek. Many, many times had Dave seen that sign in his friend. It meant that Freddy Farmer was well nigh on fire with curiosity and excitement.

"It worked, Dave, it worked!" finally came the faint whisper to Dawson's ears. "It's going along just as we hoped it would."

"As far as that door, anyway," Dave grunted, as a familiar eerie tingling sensation came to the back of his neck. "But what happens on the other side of that door is in the lap of the gods, if you get what I mean. I.... Hey! Serrangi isn't around any more!"

"No, I know it," Freddy said. "While you were reading the note his nibs went through the door we're supposed to go through."

"Yeah?" Dave echoed and scowled down into his coffee cup. "I sure hope he didn't go out to sharpen up his knife. I think I would have liked it better if Serrangi had acted as postman instead of that throat slitting customer. I never did like a middle man in things; a go-between. However, there's nothing that can be done about it, now. We follow through, of course?"

"Of course!" came the English youth's quick reply. "I wouldn't miss this for the world!"

Dave smiled in spite of himself. The remark was typical of Freddy Farmer. He was the kind who might jump ten feet if a mouse should suddenly pop out of its hole at him, but he would step right up and paste Death right on the nose without giving it a second thought. Yes, indeed, Freddy Farmer was a man in a million to have around when you got into a tight corner. He was better than a whole regiment of soldiers on occasion.

"You would!" Dave chuckled. "Well, if a knife comes singing along, don't forget to step in front of me, mate. Or maybe you'd better step in back of me. It might come that way. Well, I guess it's five minutes. Let's go take a look at what's on the other side of that door. Luck, kid!"

"I've got my fingers crossed," the English born R.A.F. ace murmured and pushed his cup of coffee to one side with a dissatisfied motion, and got up onto his feet. "Here we go."

Slouching and weaving along so as to attract the minimum of attention, Dave and Freddy made their way past the other coffee drinkers to the rear door. In front of it Dave paused and glanced back over his shoulder at Freddy. The English youth acted as though he were more or less walking in his sleep. That is, save for a tiny spark of wild excitement that burned deep in each eye. Dave winked, half grinned, and then turned front and pushed open the door.

He stepped into a room that was pitch dark save for the faint shaft of light that cut through from the coffee shop. But in a split second or even less it really was pitch dark. Dave sensed swift movement, and the door was closed quickly in back of Freddy Farmer. Almost at the same time Dave felt a tiny prick of pain in the left side of his neck. And a voice hissed softly in his ear.

"You will stand still while you are searched! Move one muscle and my knife will plunge in deep. Do not move!"

The instructions were quite unnecessary as far as Dave was concerned. The instant he had felt the pin prick of pain in his neck he had frozen stiff. Even his heart seemed to stop beating. Like a man carved out of stone he stood there in the darkness while fingers seemed to ripple all over his body from head to toe. And not for a single instant did the needle point tip of the knife leave the side of his neck. He sensed rather than saw or heard the second figure there in the pitch darkness who was searching Freddy Farmer.

Then suddenly the pin prick of the knife point was gone and steel fingers closed over his right arm at the elbow.

"Come with me!" the hissing French voice said. "It is but a short distance."

It was at that. Dave didn't take more than a dozen steps before his "guide" halted him, turned him to face the right, and pushed open a door. Before Dave could blink, and focus his eyes to the sudden change of light, he found himself in a dimly lit room that at least smelled a little less obnoxious than the coffee room up front. It was furnished as a sort of combination sleeping quarters and business office. There was a bed in the corner, a table, a desk and a few chairs. Posters quoting market spices and coffee prices hung on the wall. And scattered about here and there were empty packing boxes and cartons that had the names of shipping ports on them from all over the world.

Dave gave all the trimmings but a fleeting glance. What caught and riveted his attention was Serrangi seated in a grease-smeared over-stuffed chair. The Sumatran looked more hideous than ever in the pale light, and the brown paper wrapped cigarette he was smoking was all of five inches long. He stared at the youths out of eyes that were expressionless as those of a dead fish. He made no move, nor sign, nor said anything. He seemed not to hear the rapid jumble of a Far Eastern tongue that hissed over Dave's shoulder. Nor did his eyes follow two figures as they glided out of the room, and softly closed the door.

He simply stared unseeing at Dave and Freddy, and Dave could feel the cold sweat begin to form in his armpits and trickle down his ribs. It was as though he and Freddy had been left standing like a couple of wooden Indians staring unspeaking at a dead man with a live cigarette in his long claw-like fingers. It was an awful feeling. Dave wanted to yell, or jump up and down. Anything to shake the evil looking Serrangi out of his trance, or whatever it was.

Suddenly an idea came to Dave. For a moment he was afraid to try it, but when Serrangi continued to stare at them out of almost sightless eyes he did so out of sheer desperation. He clicked his heels together, stiffened rigid, and flung up his right arm to the horizontal, and shouted,

"*Heil Hitler!*"

He heard the gasp of startled amazement from Freddy Farmer's lips, but he didn't waste time looking at his friend. He kept his eyes riveted on Serrangi's face, and in the next second he received his reward. The owner of the Devil's Den relaxed outwardly. Most of the fishy look left his eyes. He nodded his head slightly, and what probably was meant for a smile caused one corner of his mouth to twitch.

"You took long enough, comrade," he said in a voice that sounded like ashes sliding down a tin roof. "*Heil Hitler!* And what brings you two here to the Devil's Den? I have received no word that you were to be expected!"

The man spoke perfect German, and Dave had the sudden feeling that Serrangi had spent a long time in Berlin, as well as in a lot of other places. The Sumatran was hideous to behold, and his clothes looked not one bit cleaner nor more costly than those of any one of his coffee shop's customers. Yet, somehow, the certain something that lurked deep in the one good eye gave one the impression that the shaven, sun blackened, egg shaped head contained a brain that was as quick as a steel trap. And as deadly, too. Yes, Serrangi, of the Devil's Den, might look like the dope filled fool, but he was undoubtedly the direct opposite.

"Well?" he suddenly snarled like a Prussian officer when neither of the boys spoke. "Have you tongues? Or is it perhaps the look of my face you do not like, *hein*?"

"The fortunes of war, is the answer to your question, *mein Herr*," Freddy Farmer spoke up. "We were traveling by boat for service to *Der Fuehrer* in Australia. However, the boat was torpedoed and sunk. We were two of the few saved. By a fishing boat. It put us ashore here at Singapore. We had no choice in the matter. Our first task was to avoid the police. We...."

"You fools!" Serrangi rasped and thumped one clenched fist on the arm of his chair. "So you came here, to the Devil's Den? To the place the swine police inspect nightly, and raid at least twice a week! Have you no brains in your heads? What brand of stupid swine is *Herr Himmler* enlisting in his precious Gestapo these days. *Gott!*"

"We are sorry, *Herr* Serrangi," Dave began.

"You mean you are *lucky*!" Serrangi cut in. "Lucky that those policemen tonight were searching for a pair of petty thieves. Had it been one of their regular raids you would now be behind bars, and your hides not worth a Reich mark!"

The Devil's Den owner made a savage little gesture with one hand for emphasis. Then he leaned forward slightly and the dead fish look virtually leaped back into his eyes.

"So you came to the Devil's Den?" he murmured in a soft yet deadly tone. "And how did two on their way to Australia know of the Devil's Den? Perhaps somebody told you here in Singapore, eh? Told you that old Serrangi would look out for you, so?"

"So, there appear to be three, not two, fools in this room!"

Freddy Farmer's voice was like a machine gun going off. Dave started violently inwardly, and he watched for the look of blind rage to rush over Serrangi's ugly face. But no rage appeared. Instead the Devil's Den owner glanced at Freddy with a new interest. A new interest, and just the slightest touch of respect in his eyes.

"With a tongue like that, you must have been close to death many times in your life, my friend!" the Sumatran grunted. "But perhaps I do not understand the meaning of your words, eh?"

"The meaning was plain enough!" Freddy Farmer snapped as he thrust his chin out. "We of the Gestapo who serve the Fuehrer, and the Fatherland, unto the death, do not go about revealing who we are by stupid questions. *Mein Gott!* Do you think the Devil's Den is not known beyond the borders of Singapore? Do you think that in Berlin the name, Serrangi, has no meaning? Do you think we do not plan ahead for all eventualities? *Himmel!* We were put ashore with our money, our forged papers, and everything we carried, lost! Would you have us sit on the beach and cry great tears, and hope for the miracle of a boat coming along to pick us up and take us southward to Australia? Of course not! There was but one thing to do. We did it. We came here and identified ourselves so that we could talk with you."

"I see, I see," Serrangi murmured in an almost apologetic tone. "But more than one poor fool has thrown away his life out here because of his tongue. However, you convince me that you are not of that type. Torpedoed, eh? And going to Australia? What was to be the nature of your work in Australia?"

The Sumatran looked at Dave as he asked the question, but the Yank born R.A.F. Flight Lieutenant was not to be caught off guard that easily. He dragged down one corner of his mouth and gave Serrangi a hard stare.

"In Berlin there is one *Herr Himmler*," he said. "If you communicate with him perhaps he will be good enough to tell you of the work we were to do in Australia."

The Devil's Den owner grunted, and then his thin body shook with silent laughter.

"So!" he finally exclaimed. "So much for my curiosity, eh? It would seem that there are *no* fools in this room. And at least two who are well trained members of the Gestapo. But I am still interested about your unfortunate affair at sea. Tell me about it. Perhaps I have sailed on the same ship. Perhaps I even know her captain. Tell me about it."

# CHAPTER NINE
## *The Gods Smile*

Serrangi of the Devil's Den made the request in a very matter of fact, friend to friend tone. But it sounded alarm bells inside Dave. He suddenly knew that the next few moments could well mean life or death for Freddy and him. Their faked story had to be good. It had to be better than that. It had to be perfect. One little slip-up, one tiny flaw, and Serrangi would pounce on it like a striking vulture. It was obvious that the man was going to check and double-check every little detail with what he himself knew. And because of the high position that Serrangi undoubtedly held in the shadier circles of Singapore, he probably was well informed on everything about everything. Yes, here was the test. Here was the test of presenting the ship torpedoing knowledge with which Air Vice Marshal Bostworth had acquainted them.

Dave shrugged, made a little gesture, and without asking Serrangi permission he casually dropped into a vacant chair.

"It was not something one likes to remember," he grunted. "However, if you like to hear of such things, I see no reason why we should not tell you."

Dave shrugged again and swiveled around to look at Freddy who had followed his lead and also dropped comfortably into a chair.

"Do you wish to tell him, my friend?" Dave asked. "I was unconscious for a bit, you know. From the explosion. Perhaps something happened during that time that I miss."

"If it did, I do not remember," the English youth replied in a bored voice. "No, go ahead and tell him all about it. Then, perhaps, we can get on with more important things."

Dave made a face, hunched a shoulder, and swiveled back to face Serrangi. He scowled for a moment as though collecting his memory thoughts, then he launched into a detailed torpedoing at sea. It was really a masterpiece of description. In fact, it was almost as though Dave and Freddy had actually lived through it! Serrangi listened eagerly, and every now and then he interrupted with a pointed question. However, through the grace of God, and Dave's quick wits, the Yank was able to give a satisfactory answer to each and every question. Finally, when he was sweating inwardly from pent up nervousness, he came to the end of his bogus tale.

"And so we are here," he grunted. "And next time I hope we can go by airplane. I am not one who is happy on the sea. Any sea! So, now you know all about it. Consider yourself fortunate that you were not aboard. It was not pleasant, and we were not saved through any efforts of our own. I shall always believe that it was the great invisible hand of *Der Fuehrer* that reached out and protected us. It is not the first time in my life that I have felt that way, either."

"It was at least the will of our leader, that you should be saved," Serrangi said with almost a reverent note in his ashy voice. "But just the same it was unfortunate."

The Devil's Den owner stopped and scowled at the ash of his cigarette. For a long time he didn't say anything. Dave and Freddy, believing that silence was their best bet, didn't so much as utter a peep. They sat perfectly still looking at Serrangi with their fingers mentally crossed, and a prayer in their hearts. They had driven in the opening wedge. It was now up to Serrangi to make the next move ... if any. And that was the point! That was the thought that so completely filled their heads they felt ready to explode from the pressure.

Would Serrangi take them into his crowd? Would he assign them to some espionage work here in Singapore and give them the stepping stone they needed to attain their real objective? Or would he simply express sorrow at their plight, but state that it was not up to him to take care of two stranded Gestapo agents? But, perhaps more important than anything else, *did Serrangi believe their story*? He acted as though he did, but that could mean most anything. And, likewise, nothing. What thoughts were passing through that brain of his behind the hideous face? Was he sealing their doom ... or what?

As the silence continued it was all Dave could do to refrain from encouraging the Sumatran to speak. It was almost as though he had sunk back into the weird trance he'd been in when they first entered the room. His face was a blank, save for the frown. And the fishy look was creeping back into his eyes again. Then, suddenly, Freddy Farmer took the bull by the horns.

"Well, I can see we were mistaken!" he said harshly. "There is no help to be had here. I believe I'll remember that fact when I do return to Berlin!"

"Sit down, or there'll be a knife in your heart!"

Serrangi's voice was like the hiss of a deadly snake coiled to strike. His eyes seemed to flash sparks as he fixed them on Freddy Farmer. And one hand darted under his dirty jacket like a little shaft of lightning. Freddy managed to glare but he sat down very quickly.

"That is better," Serrangi said in a softer voice. "Listen to me, you of the quick tongue! In Germany you may be lord and master over many slaves, but here in Singapore *Serrangi* holds a man's life or his death in his hands. Remember that! Your Fuehrer may be the greatest man ever born. I truly believe he is. But it is not my love for Germany, or your Fuehrer's cause that makes me work for you Nazis. It is the price you *pay me*. I am only interested in wealth, and my own power. So do not speak your sharp Nazi tongue to me. I will not crawl. Instead I will slit your throat and throw you to the street dogs, and forget all about you by the morrow."

The owner of the Devil's Den nodded curtly for emphasis, and made a little motion with one hand as though brushing something aside.

"And now that we understand each other," he continued after the pause. "We can talk of things to do. First, it will be impossible for me to arrange for you to continue your journey to Australia. There is not a boat leaving Singapore these days that you could possibly hide on. And...."

"But as passengers?" Dave grunted to add to the impression that they really were Australia bound.

"Even more impossible!" the Sumatran grated at him. "The British would unmask you in five minutes. No, I cannot help you at all to continue to Australia."

"Then, perhaps, here in Singapore?" Freddy Farmer murmured with a world of genuine hopefulness in his voice. "Perhaps you have work for us? It does not matter where one serves, so long as one serves the Fatherland."

Serrangi shook his head and took a fresh cigarette from a carved ivory box on the desk.

"There are too many of you Nazi agents in Singapore, as it is," he grunted. "The dog British are not stupid all day *and* night. They feel war in the Far

East is not far off, and their Intelligence Service is on the alert. No, I could not give you anything to do in Singapore that would make you even worth your food and drink. It was indeed most unfortunate that you were torpedoed at sea."

Serrangi nodded and sighed as though that ended everything. Dave's heart dropped down into his paper thin soled shoes, and so did Freddy Farmer's. It was as though the gods had kidded them along this far just for the added pleasure of slapping them down just a hair's breadth short of the mark. If Serrangi tossed them out, there would be nothing to do but go back to Air Vice Marshal Bostworth and report complete failure. And the suspected deadly menace that was creeping slowly but surely around the British in the Far East would remain as much of a mystery as ever.

"Well, that is the way with war!" Dave said in a bitter voice that was far from all sham.

"True words you speak," Serrangi said almost kindly. "Who are we to pick and choose, and say when and how we will accomplish a task? But there is no room for you here in Singapore. If only you were Luftwaffe pilots, then that would be a different matter."

Both Dave and Freddy came close to falling off their chairs in stunned amazement at the man's words. They stared wide eyed at him as though they could not, or did not dare, trust their ears. It was Dave who found his tongue first.

"If *we* were Luftwaffe pilots?" he cried. "Why do you say that?"

"There is a task," Serrangi said with a shrug. "But the men must be able to fly airplanes. True there is one here in Singapore who could do the task. But he cannot leave his post. Rather he would undo much that has been prepared, if he were to do so."

"It is the will of *Der Fuehrer* again!" Freddy Farmer cried wildly and sprang to his feet. "*Heil Hitler!* His thoughts are always with one and all. You are always in the Leader's heart. Serrangi! Look at us. Your wish has been granted. Your desire has been fulfilled!"

The Sumatran looked, but the expression on his face was like that of a man waiting for the rabbits to come popping out of the high silk hat.

"More words!" he finally snapped. "What do you mean, my loud mouthed friend?"

"*Der Fuehrer's* solution of your problem!" Freddy cried and pointed to Dave and then at himself. "My friend and I are seasoned veterans of the great and glorious Luftwaffe. Not until after Crete were we assigned full time duty under*Herr* Himmler. *Gott!* Fly airplanes? My new found friend, we can do that in our sleep. So you see? It is the Leader's will that we be given work to do for him, though we cannot continue our journey to Australia!"

"But absolutely!" Dave shouted, taking the cue from Freddy Farmer. "Fly airplanes? The joy of my life. And after all, it is not an impossible flight from here to Australia, given the correct plane."

A happy look that had gradually spread over Serrangi's face as the two boys "raved" was suddenly banished by a look of sharp annoyance.

"Impossible!" he grated. "The flight that must be made is in the opposite direction. To the north. Besides, there is more than *Herr* Hitler's desires connected with the matter. But this is true? You two are airplane pilots?"

"But of course!" Dave shouted right back at him. "And my comrade here is one of Germany's greatest. He has been decorated by *Der Fuehrer's* own hand. It was for unbelievable gallantry in the Norway campaign. But, a flight to the north, you say? Why to the north? And what is the task that is to be undertaken?"

"You suggested I communicate with Berlin!" Serrangi snarled with heavy sarcasm. "Perhaps it would be a good idea for you to communicate with Tokio!"

Dave felt as though he had suddenly been slapped across the face with a bolt of lightning. In spite of his efforts his eyes flew open wide with amazement. In a flash, though, he realized his mistake and hastened to cover it up.

"Tokio?" he breathed eagerly. "So it is to come *soon*, eh? So perhaps it will not be a complete loss if my friend and I do not reach Australia. After all, it seems that the tasks are connected."

A bright light shot through Serrangi's eyes, and he gave Dave a searching look that seemed to probe right into his brain.

"So that was the kind of work you would do in Australia, eh?" he murmured. "But, of course. Berlin and Tokio are working together. And the fat fool in Rome thumps his chest, and shouts stupid things to his stupid soldiers. Well, this is all very different. Much, much different."

Serrangi paused and nodded his head, and came as close to beaming with pleasure as it was possible for a man with his face to do so. Dave and Freddy practically hung on the edges of their chairs waiting for the Sumatran to say more. But when the words finally did come they dashed high hopes back down again on the cold, cold ground.

"I do not know the details of the task," the Devil's Den owner said. "I only know that there is a task to be accomplished. That there is a flight to be made to the north. And I also know this!"

The man stopped abruptly and fastened the two youths with a steady stare.

"I know that it may mean death even before the flight is begun!" he snapped.

"We are not dead, yet," Dave said with true Nazi bravado, and airily waved a hand. "And for that matter, neither of us expects to be dead for a long, long time to come. But if you know nothing of the details...?"

Dawson let the rest trail off significantly, and waited.

"No, I know nothing of the details," Serrangi said. "But I do know where the details are to be obtained. Two streets north of where we are, now, there is a small rug merchant's shop on the corner. The name on the hanging sign is Agiz Ammarir. I will give you a coin presently. You will go to the rug merchant's shop, ask for Agiz Ammarir. There will be a native girl who greets you at the door. Tell her that you have a bill to settle. She will summon Agiz Ammarir. When he appears give him the coin. The coin will tell him all he wants to know. From him you will learn more of what is to be done. What *must* be done ... and soon!"

The man almost shouted the last. His face clouded with fury and he smashed both clenched fists down on the arms of the chair. The cold anger in his eyes caused a tiny shiver to ripple up and down Dave's spine. Here indeed was the real Serrangi coming to the surface. The savage beast within him breaking through the thin veneer of civilization in which he cloaked his true self. Dave thought of being a helpless prisoner in the hands of a man like Serrangi, and the very thought made his blood run cold.

"Have no doubts about us, Serrangi," Dave heard Freddy Farmer speak up. "If it can be done, we will do it."

The Devil's Den owner snorted through his thin hawk-beak nose and flung the English youth a withering glance.

"I know all about your Nazi boasts!" he snapped. "But the Far East is not Germany. And Singapore is not your Berlin where you can demand the help of any man on the street, whether it costs his life or not. But it is I who talks too much, now. Enough! Here is the coin you will give to Agiz Ammarir. Leave here within the next fifteen minutes and go to his rug shop. Perhaps we shall meet again. But, whether we do or not ... *Heil Hitler!*"

Both youths sprang to their feet and returned the Nazi Party cry and salute. Serrangi shrugged and then waved them away as though they were two pieces of merchandise in which he was no longer interested. As they stepped outside the door into the hall of pitch darkness, two shapes materialized at their side, took them each by the arm and silently led them to the door of the coffee shop. When they passed through into the dim, smoke filled room their two escorts melted back into the darkness. Ignoring a few questioning glances that were cast their way, Dave led the way to their vacated table, started to slump down in his chair, but checked himself and gave Freddy a meaning look.

"Why drink more of this poison?" he growled in thick French. "Let us go somewhere else, eh?"

The English youth nodded glumly, and the pair slouched nonchalantly toward the front door.

Dave Dawson

## CHAPTER TEN
### *The Touch of Death*

In the matter of a few seconds Dave and Freddy were once more out in Bukum Street. The street of a million different smells and all bad. Nevertheless, after the inside of the Devil's Den both boys stopped and dragged night air deep into their lungs.

"Sweet tripe, I know my nose will never be the same again!" Dave muttered. "Imagine spending a whole evening in that place. I wouldn't be surprised but what that's the answer to the mysterious disappearance of Bostworth's agent."

"What do you mean by that?" Freddy asked as the pair started moving slowly up the street.

"The poor devil probably had to spend four or five hours in that stink hole, and just naturally passed out cold," Dave said. "They got scared and threw his body in the harbor, and he drowned. No fooling! I feel like I'd been drugged for a year."

"Well, we're out of the horrible place, anyway," Freddy said. Then after a short silence, he said, "Darnedest thing ever, wasn't it, Dave?"

The American youth grunted, and shrugged, but didn't reply directly. He walked along in brooding silence.

"Well, was it anything like you expected?" Freddy demanded when no comment by his friend seemed forthcoming. "Was it, I ask?"

"Yes, and no," Dave said. "I mean, I went into that place expecting anything. Fact is, Freddy, if you must know, I'm just a wee bit worried about these last couple of hours. They passed off smooth as silk. Too smooth, I'm thinking."

"Good Lord!" the English youth gasped. "Do you think Serrangi is wise to us? But.... But that doesn't make sense, Dave!"

"You tell me one thing about our war experiences that *did* make sense *at* the time!" Dave said. "Now don't get me wrong. I don't mean that we fell flat on our faces as far as convincing Serrangi that we're Nazi agents. If he had suspected us at all, found any flaw in our story, you and I would have sharp steel in us right now. No, I honestly think we put our story over okay. But I don't think scar faced Serrangi took it hook, line and sinker. After all, Freddy, that bird has to play a very slick game or his name will be mud in nothing flat. I.... Darn it, Freddy, I have a feeling that the test isn't over by any manner or means."

"You mean Serrangi is passing us along to this Agiz Ammarir for his inspection and approval?" Freddy suggested.

Dave hunched his shoulders and made a clucking sound with his tongue.

"Could be," he said. "Something like that, I think. There's one thing, and it's this. Serrangi is pretty much burned up about not getting action on something big. Something that has to do with a mysterious plane flight to the north. And does the guy mean a flight to Tokio, I wonder? Anyway, he wasn't play acting at the last. He was plenty sore. And, brother, I wouldn't want any guy like that to get sore at me. Slicing your ears and nose off would be just a warm-up for his type. And there's another thing that struck me as queer, too."

"Such as?" Freddy Farmer encouraged when Dave lapsed into another spell of brooding silence.

"His not knowing anything of the details of this mysterious flight," Dave murmured after a long pause. "If he's the paid Nazi agent big shot in this part of the world, you'd think he'd know everything about what's planned as well as what's taking place. Don't you figure it that way, too?"

"Yes, I guess I do," Freddy Farmer replied slowly. "But I got the impression, Dave, that this flight to the north in a plane is not all Nazi. I have a very good feeling there's more Tokio to it than Berlin. And, by the way, you carried off that secret work in Australia top-hole, Dave, old fellow."

"Thanks, and I sure hope so," Dave said in a fervent voice. "But I hope this Agiz Ammarir doesn't get too curious about it. And.... Holy smoke!"

"What, Dave?" Freddy gasped in alarm as Dawson stopped short and gulped.

"Wouldn't it be just too, too ducky if that's what Serrangi is checking up!" Dave groaned. "Supposing this Ammarir knows all about Nazi work in Australia, and is going to pass on us for Scar Face! Freddy, don't look right now, but I think you and I are walking the rim of a volcano that's liable to ring the gong on us at any moment. Yeah! I don't think I ever wanted to see tomorrow's sun as much as I do tonight. But.... Oh, what the heck! A fellow can't live forever, so why worry?"

"You mean by that that we should of course carry on, don't you?" Freddy asked.

"Heck, yes!" Dawson snorted. "It's a mess all around, but there's only one thing to be done about it. Stay in there and keep pitching. To use that Nazi boast I pulled on Serrangi, we're not dead men, yet. But it certainly would have helped a lot if Bostworth had known just what he was shooting at. After all, he just about gave us zero-minus to work on. True, the Devil's Den tip looks like it might get us some results. But that's just the idea. What *kind* of results?"

"Quite," Freddy murmured. Then as though in justified defense of one of his countrymen, he said, "If Bostworth had known a lot, Dave, he wouldn't have needed us at all. I really take it as an honor that he selected us to help him in this mess."

"Oh, sure, sure, me too," Dave hastened to soothe his friend's feelings. "Don't mind me. You should know me better than that. I'm just the beefing kind. Heck! I wouldn't quit now even if Air Vice Marshal Bostworth should suddenly pop out of one of these shacks and order me off the job. And you know it, pal. So stop ribbing me."

"Then use that big mouth for talking sense only," the English youth growled. Then after giving Dave's arm a quick squeeze of friendship, he said, "I think there's one thing we should do, Dave. I've got a feeling. Sort of one of your famous hunches, you might say."

"Let's have it, my little man," Dave said. "I'm all ears."

"Yes, I know, and big ones at that," Freddy Farmer came right back at him. "Seriously speaking, though, Dave. If we're to pose as a couple of Nazi agents, let's try to actually feel that we are. I mean, when you do a thing by halfway measures you sometimes bump into more trouble than if you made no effort at all to act a part."

"Okay, by me, Herr Fritz von Farmer," Dave whispered with a chuckle as they reached the first of the cross streets. "From here in we're more German than old Uncle Goering."

"I mean it, Dave!" Freddy said grimly. "We don't know what kind of a trap we're walking into. One slip of the tongue, when either of us is not thinking, and it might be curtains for both of us. *Think* that you're a German, Dave. Make yourself *feel* it! I can't put it into words, but.... Well, blast it, I simply sort of sense something in the air. Like a coming storm, or something."

"Okay!" Dave said gently. "I'll be as dumb as any Hun you ever saw, my boy. But lay off this hunch stuff. That's my racket, pal!"

Freddy didn't make any reply to that crack and the two youths walked along Bukum Street in silence. Every now and then a native or two glided past, and every so often they passed an open shop out of which poured the babble of high keyed voices. As they neared the corner of the second street on which they would find Agiz Ammarir's rug shop the lights became less and less until they were walking along in more or less murky darkness.

And when they were but fifty yards from the single electric lighted sign of the rug merchant ... it happened!

Dave sensed rather than saw movement on Freddy's right. But he did hear the sound of swift movement, and as he automatically half spun and grabbed for his friend he saw the dull gleam of a long bladed knife that seemed to hang poised directly over the English youth's head.

A wild cry of alarm rose up to Dave's lips, but for some reason he didn't spill it off. Perhaps it was because by then he was in the middle of wild furious action. In what was really one continuous movement he thrust one hand against Freddy's shoulder, kicked out a foot to trip his friend and send him spilling to the sidewalk, and lashed out blindly with his other clenched fist. White pain streaking from his knuckles clear up to his shoulder socket gave him the wild satisfaction of knowing he had hit human bone and flesh.

Then in the next instant he had leaped over Freddy's squirming body on the sidewalk and was slamming out with both fists, and connecting with a shadowy figure that screamed with alarm and pain. That there was still a knife some place didn't even occur to Dave. That his pal, Freddy Farmer, had come within a few short inches of being killed was the one and only thing uppermost in his mind. And for that reason alone he fought with the fury of a cornered jungle tiger.

But it was all over almost as soon as it had started. Dave was in the act of closing his fingers about a greasy wrist when the shadowy figure let out one last cry of pain and virtually vanished away in thin air. Hardly realizing what he was doing, Dave bent over, scooped up a steel bladed knife that lay at his feet on the sidewalk, and hurled it after the shadow in the darkness. And, then suddenly, as he stood there trembling with rage, he realized that his lips were spitting curses at the fleeing shadow in perfect Hamburg German. The realization was so startling that he cut himself off in the middle of a word and stood motionless. Reaction took that moment to set in and he began trembling like a leaf. He was unable to stop himself until Freddy Farmer managed to scramble up and grip him hard on the arm.

"Are you all right?" Freddy Farmer muttered in German.

"Fit as can be," Dave grunted and gave a little shake of his head. "Did you hear me, Freddy. Boy! Was I pouring out the old German, and not even realizing it. Talk about taking you at your word!"

"As you would say, they don't make them any more perfect than you," Freddy whispered and pressed Dave's arm again. "I fancy that's about the umpteenth time you've saved my life since we first met."

"Nuts!" Dave growled good naturedly. "Save *your* life? Where do you get that stuff? I let fly because I thought the guy's knife was headed for *my* throat. A fine lot of money that hold-up lug would have found on us, huh?"

"*If* he was looking for money!" Freddy Farmer grunted and scowled around at the darkness. "It could be for a very different reason, you know."

"Nuts again!" Dave snapped. "You're cutting out paper dolls, Freddy. Serrangi, you mean? He wouldn't have waited this long, pal. Forget it! That lad was just hoping to pick up a little small change. The knife was just to help him do it quicker. Come on, let's get going. Maybe he's got a pal hanging around. I'm just One Punch Dawson, you know. Next time I'd probably be the one that got clouted. Come on."

Freddy Farmer mumbled something and dropped into step. They walked the last fifty yards a little faster and finally came to a halt before Agiz Ammarir's door. There was light inside but the glass was so dirty and covered with rugs hung up for display they couldn't see inside. Dave hesitated, took a deep breath, swallowed hard, and jerked the bell cord. The echo of a pleasing tingling came to them through the door. Presently a shadow appeared on the other side, and a moment later the door was pulled open.

Dave opened his mouth to speak to the girl, but not a sound left his lips because it was not a native girl who stood holding the door open. It was Serrangi, instead, and Dave's eyes bugged out as he and Freddy Farmer both stared in speechless amazement.

## CHAPTER ELEVEN
### *Flight to the North*

"Serrangi!" Dave finally gulped out. "*Mein Gott!* What kind of trick is this you play?"

The owner of the Devil's Den smiled crookedly, opened the door wider and nodded them in.

"Come inside, my friends," he said. "It is sometimes necessary to be more than one person. I believed this was one of them. But come inside before the whole waterfront sees us chattering here. Seat yourselves in those chairs and be comfortable."

Very much like two awed kids being led through Toyland for the first time, Dave Dawson and Freddy Farmer stepped into the room, and slowly seated themselves in a couple of chairs. The shop was filled with rugs of all sizes, and makes, and all colors. They were on the floor in piles, hung four and five deep on the walls, and suspended on rollers from the ceiling. Agiz Ammarir's rug shop looked as though it could supply the whole world, alone, for the next couple of years. It did not, however, give either Dave or Freddy that impression, for the simple reason that their entire attention was riveted on Serrangi. Silent and wide eyed, they watched him close the door, bolt and lock it, and then move over to a chair for himself. In return, though, he didn't give them so much as a single glance. Once seated, he set about lighting one of his long brown paper wrapped cigarettes, with both his good and bad eye fixed expressionlessly on space.

Not until he was spewing smoke ceilingward did he lower his gaze and take further notice of their presence.

"You are entitled to an explanation, so I will give you one," he said in his sifting ashes voice. "In these days, the man who takes anything on face value is a fool. And the man who trusts even his own brother may well be dead tomorrow. For that reason I told you to come here to speak with one Agiz Ammarir. For that reason I had one of my men make a show of waylaying you and killing you en route. I...."

"So that was a fake?" Dave gasped out in German. "But that knife was inches from my friend's throat!"

"It would never have descended all the way to his throat," Serrangi said placidly. "The attack was to learn what you would say on the impulse of the moment. *And in what language!* There was once a man who came to see me with a promise of great wealth for me ... if I would reveal a little of the many things I know. He, too, presented himself as a German and a loyal follower of Herr Hitler. But I am not the one to be taken in that easy. I sent him, also, to visit Agiz Ammarir. He too, was attacked on the way. He opened his mouth, and in so doing sealed his doom, for he *cried out in English*. He was, of course, a British Secret Service agent. I have never seen him since. I suppose the poor fellow died from the shock of the attack."

The Devil's Den owner gave a little shrug and wave of his hand. Dave stared at him with admiration in his eyes, but the look was forced, for in his heart Dave felt only loathing, disgust, and cold anger for the man. So that was how Air Vice Marshal Bostworth's agent disappeared? God bless Freddy Farmer for his sudden hunch about thinking as well as acting as a German. If it hadn't been for Freddy he might have let go a few choice words in English, himself. And then he and Freddy would have mysteriously disappeared. A deadly snake if one ever crawled. That indeed was Serrangi, of the Devil's Den. Deadly, and clever, too. He knew what had happened to Bostworth's agent all right. Ten to one he had killed the man with his own hand when the attacker had reported that English had been cried out. But Serrangi was clever enough not to admit as much. No, not even to a pair who seemingly had proved they were a couple of Adolf Hitler's own paid killers.

"And so, it was only good sense for me to test you two in the same manner," Serrangi's voice broke into Dave's thoughts. "Of course I felt certain of you, but it was best to make sure. So, enough of this kind of talk. Let us speak of other things. The flight that must be made to the north for one thing. But first, have you two flown in this part of the world?"

Dave was tempted to lie, but on second thought decided that for once the truth might serve them better.

"No," he said just as Freddy started shaking his head. "We have done all our flying in Europe. But why is it important we have experience flying here in the Far East?"

"It is not important," Serrangi said. "It might perhaps be a bit helpful if you knew some of the country out here. That, however, is only a matter of opinion. I do not fly, but I suppose that flying is much the same in any part of the world?"

"Depends on the pilot," Freddy Farmer spoke up, and let it go at that.

"Of course," Serrangi grunted, and drew a roll of paper from inside his jacket. "Here," he continued, "is a map of this part of the world. As you will see it is well marked, and contains much data that one would not find on other maps of the same section of the world. Here, have a good look at it."

Serrangi unrolled a fair sized map and handed it to Dave. The American R.A.F. Flight Lieutenant took it in hands difficult to keep from trembling. Then he swiveled around a bit in his chair, and held it so that Freddy could look at it too. They did that little thing together and within two split seconds their hearts were hammering with suppressed excitement, to say nothing of amazement. The map was of the entire Malay Peninsula, Thailand, Burma, and a part of China as far north as Chungking. It was indeed a fine map. It was a perfect map for a pilot, because it contained countless little bits of information a pilot would like to know when flying over any of the territory. In fact, the information had been jotted down by some one who was obviously a pilot. And when Dave peered hard at the countless little margin notes and signs a cold lump of lead seemed to form in his stomach, and there was a great sickness in his brain. Beyond all question the person who had made the notes and signs was expertly acquainted with the way in which R.A.F. navigation maps are marked. In short, no less than an R.A.F. pilot had prepared this map he and Freddy Farmer stared at.

"It was a pilot who made this map, was it not?" Freddy Farmer suddenly shot out the question.

Serrangi beamed and looked very pleased.

"So you *are* pilots, so?" he murmured. "That was not just Nazi boasting to get you to give me work? Fine! Yes, it was made by a pilot. One of your own kind in England's flying service, it may interest you to know. He has been of great value to your Fuehrer out here. He will be a great hero when he returns to your homeland."

"Perhaps we know him," Dave murmured in a half interested sort of way.

The lead didn't draw Serrangi out any, however. The Devil's Den owner shrugged and made a little gesture with his half smoked cigarette.

"It is possible," he grunted. "But we do not speak names out here. Have you not noticed I have not even asked your names? I do not care to know them. Then nothing can make me reveal them to anybody else, you see? Who a man is, is nothing. What he can do, and does, is everything. A name is but another unnecessary detail you have to keep alive in your brain. Too many details is a bad thing. But, yes, that is a pilot's map. You think you could fly by it?"

"Why not?" Dave echoed.

"It is clear enough for a blind man to read," Freddy Farmer added. "Where do you want us to fly?"

Serrangi smiled and lifted both hands palms showing outward in a slow down and stop gesture.

"Let us obtain the plane first," he said.

The words fell like thunderbolts on Dave and Freddy. They stared at him out of incredulous eyes.

"You mean, you have no plane?" Dave eventually demanded.

"And where would I keep a plane here on Singapore Island!" the other snarled at him. "Of course I have no plane! Did I not say that there was more than a little risk attached to this highly important task?"

"But if we are to fly a plane?" Freddy Farmer said, and then let a perfect expression of Teutonic dumbness of his face say the rest.

"Steal one from the British!" Serrangi snapped at him. "It has been done before, and it can be done again. And, of course, you would steal one that is fully armed and contains sufficient fuel for a long flight."

Dave tapped the map with a finger.

"To Chungking?" he asked.

Serrangi thought that was very funny, and laughed shrilly.

"No, not to Chungking!" he finally cried and wiped his eyes with the back of his hand. "It is the Japanese with whom we work, not the Chinese. No, the end of the flight will be to the point that is marked there on the map near Lashio, in Burma."

Dave and Freddy glanced down quickly at the map. A little Burmese mountain village called Raja, just east of Lashio, was marked with a red circled black cross. Dave heard Freddy catch his breath, and he started inwardly with excitement, himself, because at Lashio was the beginning of the famous Burma Road, fighting China's lifeline. Her one remaining supply route contact with the outside world. And the whole world knew that the one thing the little brown rats of the bucktoothed Jap emperor on his white horse wanted to do most was cut the Burma Road. Once they did that they could starve the gallant Chinese into an armistice in short order. And once China had fallen, hordes upon hordes of Japanese lice could be sent elsewhere for more conquests.

For two long minutes Dave stared down at the map, then he slowly raised his eyes to Serrangi's face and smiled slyly.

"So, the Burma Road, ja?" he muttered. "*Herr* Hitler will be most pleased. It will open a way into India, perhaps."

The Devil's Den owner snorted and waved the statement aside as though it were small time stuff.

"The small beginning of many things," he said. "When the guns and air bombs of Nippon start thundering on the given day half the Eastern world will not live to learn what happened! But, at Raja is the beginning of everything. At Raja the signal will be given. I have arranged everything here at Singapore. We cannot possibly fail if those at Raja do their part. The British! They are so sure of themselves. Such great confidence in their mighty navy! Well, the time has come to teach the British Lion that others have learned the trick of gaining power. But I do not need to tell you about England. Your Fuehrer knows all about England, and how to handle her."

Dave was sorely tempted to shout, "Sure! Like his cockeyed Luftwaffe tried to handle her last September, hey?" but of course he breathed not a word. Instead he nodded his head and looked very wise and self satisfied ... and waited, seething inside with anger.

"For weeks," Serrangi went on, "I have been maintaining contact with the secret Japanese headquarters at Raja, by airplane, and radio. No, the plane has not been mine. My friend serving with the Royal Air Force here at

Singapore, but with a prayer for England's complete defeat in his heart. He has taken the information I have given him and flown with it far out to sea when on what you call, solo patrol. At a certain rendezvous he has contacted a Japanese submarine and dropped the information to the water. From the submarine the information has been radioed to Tokio, and from there southward to Raja. But I dare not trust that method any longer."

"You don't trust this ... this R.A.F. pilot?" Dave asked as the other paused.

"No, not him," Serrangi said with a laugh. "He would not dare! I hold his life between my thumb and forefinger as I might hold a wingless fly. It is the British I do not trust. They know that trouble is coming from Japan. They don't know when, and I do not believe there is an Englishman in all Singapore who so much as dreams *how close* that time is! Nevertheless they have become very much more on the alert. From one hour to the next I am not sure if my flying friend will be caught, or continue to work unhindered. And the British are watching the seas with eyes of eagles, these days. They might sink the very submarine to which my flying friend had dropped the vital information. And there is but one more set of information figures to send to Raja. They cover everything here in the Far East. I cannot run the risk that they might become lost."

"So we are to steal a plane and fly them to Raja?" Freddy Farmer spoke up as the Sumatran fell silent. "Is that what we are to do?"

"That is what you are to do!" Serrangi said with a short nod. "You will steal a plane and escape to Raja. When you arrive you will be treated as great heroes. I can assure you of that. Any honor you desire will be yours. And I ... I will have triple the wealth of any man in Singapore for my reward."

"It can be done," Dave grunted. Then giving the Devil's Den owner a keen look. "One thing, though. My Fuehrer's teaching compels me to make sure of all things. You say you cannot run the risk of the information becoming lost. Supposing we fail to steal a plane? Supposing we are caught? What then, eh?"

Serrangi smiled, and indeed it was the smile of Satan's own son.

"I should have added, *and not know it*," the Sumatran said. "If you fail and are caught, I shall know it almost at the same instant. Then I shall have to find another way."

"But the information!" Freddy Farmer cried in true German bewilderment. "What if it falls into the hands of the British?"

"The very least of my worries, for it is no worry at all," Serrangi replied promptly. "It would do them no good. It would give them headaches, and it would probably drive them mad in the end. But they would never be able to decipher what it meant. That, my two friends, is why Serrangi holds the position he does. No man alive can read my code without the key. And only *one* other man knows the key at a time!"

Dave frowned, started to ask what that meant, and then the truth of the statement hit him right between the eyes. To be given Serrangi's code key was to be handed your death warrant. When you had served his evil purpose, no matter what it might be, you died ... and the next man in Serrangi's death and blood dealings was given the key.

"The one who knows the key now is at Raja?" Dave grunted.

"That is so," the Sumatran said. "And one of the Japanese Emperor's most trusted generals. To him I gave it personally. And I know the thoughts that fill your mind, now. When I have closed my work, my business, with him? Perhaps, and perhaps not. When the Japanese take Singapore there must be some one to govern and rule. Perhaps I will tire of operating the Devil's Den. Who knows ... but myself? But enough of this talk. Our work is not yet done."

Serrangi gave a wave of his hand to dismiss the loose talk, and for a moment frowned at the thread of grey smoke that spiralled upward from his cigarette. Then suddenly he nodded as though he had made up his mind on something.

"There are many Royal Air Force fields here in Singapore," he grunted. "Perhaps, though, it would be best to steal your plane from the Municipal Airport which the Government has taken over. I happen to know that it is not so well guarded as the others."

"What about the planes there?" Dave asked in a voice he had to fight to keep steady. "We would want nothing bigger than a two seater. To steal a bomber would be impossible. Too much to do before taking it off."

"There is no need to worry!" Serrangi said a bit sharply. "There are planes of all types at the Municipal Airport. And the fools ... they keep them all lined up in rows, as though they had them on display for sale. I do not feel that you will have much difficulty. True, there are armed guards about the field. But you two have heard the sound of rifles and machine guns shooting at you before now, eh?"

"More often than not," Dave said as the cold lumps of lead started rolling around in his stomach. "But when do we steal this plane? When do we make the flight? And...?"

Dave stopped as Serrangi whipped up one hand in a curt signal to shut up.

"If you will stop that chatter of the jungle monkeys, I will give you complete instructions!" the Sumatran grated. "First, the attempt should be made just before dawn, during the darkest hour of the night. Second, you will receive a certain amount of assistance from my men. They will do what they can to attract the attention of the field guards while you steal the plane. Third, be sure you steal an airplane that is well marked with R.A.F. insignia."

"Why not any plane?" Freddy Farmer wanted to know as Serrangi paused for breath.

"For very good reasons!" came the curt reply. "All civilian flying has been stopped between here and Burma. If you stole a civilian plane your position would be immediately reported by any official who sighted you. Also, you would get into trouble if you came upon British Air Force planes on patrol. Flying an R.A.F. plane, however, would not attract their attention. Now, of course, when you once get into the air you are to head in the *opposite* direction to your real objective. You will fly south toward Java until you have reached an altitude where you cannot be seen from below. You will then double back and fly up the middle of the South China Sea until you have reached the southern tip of French Indo-China. Then follow the coast northwest to Thailand, and then north to your destination."

The Sumatran stopped short, leaned forward and touched a bony finger to the map Dave and Freddy held between them.

"Study that map, and learn it well," he said. "The course is well marked on it. A course that should take you safely past all spots of possible trouble. Study also the markings of the terrain about Raja. If you have never been to Raja, it is a village of perhaps twenty bamboo huts. It is completely surrounded by wild country where no white man could survive for long. I have been told that from an airplane you cannot see a patch of ground level enough for a man to lie down on. High mountains, deep valleys, and jungle filled gorges. But there *is* flat ground there. An area big enough for five hundred airplanes to use. The Japanese have made it so, in secret. But you would never be able to find the place in a hundred years ... without this map. See where the mountain range coming down from the north meets the one that extends straight across Burma? See the blue mark made on the map? That is the spot where you will land when you have given your signal, and have received a signal in return."

"Signals?" Dave prompted as Serrangi paused again.

"Certainly," the Sumatran replied and flung him a scornful look. "You will circle the spot five times ... no more and no less ... to let General Kashomia know that you come from me. You will circle around at six thousand feet exactly. A red flare will be your order to come lower. Other flares will be fired to show you where to land on the hidden field. You will be escorted straight to General Kashomia when you have landed, and your plane has stopped. But, mark you well! Do just as I am directing you; do not make any mistakes when you reach this spot. Guns will be trained on you, and at General Kashomia's orders they could shoot you and your plane into small pieces in the matter of split seconds. Now, you have further questions before we get under way?"

"Get under way?" Freddy Farmer echoed sharply. "You mean now, this night?"

"And why not?" Serrangi demanded suspiciously. "The sooner you deliver my report to General Kashomia, the sooner the blow can be struck. Yes, tonight! Within two hours I shall see that you are taken as close to the Municipal Airport as is possible. It will then be the darkest hour, and the risk of being caught will be less. But, you object?"

"Of course not!" Dave spoke up quickly before Freddy could say anything. "But there is one thing that makes me very curious. This friend of yours who is a pilot and wears the uniform of the Royal Air Force. It is a great honor for whoever makes this flight. I am curious why your friend ... who has obviously spent so much time making this map ... does not desire the honor."

"He does," Serrangi replied with a sly grin. "He would give most anything for me to send him to Raja. But I cannot do that. His place is here. There is a great work for him to do. He...."

The Sumatran paused to chuckle, and then leaned forward in a confidential attitude.

"I will suggest a request you make to General Kashomia as part of your reward," he said. "Ask that you be allowed to fly in one of his bombing planes on the day the blow falls. When you come over Singapore you will see a sight no man may ever see again. The approach of the first Japanese bomber will be the signal for my R.A.F. friend. Everything is planned. His hand will push a cleverly hidden detonating plunger and the buried fuel stores here on Singapore Island, the ammunition stores, the hidden water reservoirs, and many other things will explode in one blinding flash that will make Singapore shake from one end of the Island to the other. Yes, from the very hangars of R.A.F. Base my friend will push the plunger that will.... But why try to describe the sight it will be? There are not enough words. However, I suggest that you request General Kashomia to let you view the sight from a Japanese bomber in the air. It will be something you will never forget. Something to tell your Fuehrer when you return to Germany in triumph. And now, get what rest you can, and study well that map. Meanwhile I will fetch you food and drink to sustain your strength during the journey ahead."

Dave just nodded as the Sumatran glanced questioningly at him and rose to his feet. Words he might say gagged in his throat. His head whirled in an invisible mass of white flame, and every ounce of blood seemed to drain from his body. The words that had passed from Serrangi's lips during the last half hour, or so, were so stunning, so brain numbing that he could hardly force thoughts to register. It was like something he might be reading out of a book thriller. Not something that was to happen in real life. It couldn't be ... but it was. Doom, terrible certain doom, hovered over Britain's mighty armed outpost of Singapore. Hovered above it to come crashing down when a certain Japanese general at Raja, in Burma, gave the signal.

"It can't happen!" Dave said fiercely to himself as Serrangi glided past him toward the rear of the rug shop. "Dear God, please, it mustn't happen!"

## CHAPTER TWELVE
### *Wings of Chaos*

Dave pressed himself flat to the ground, and dug his fingers into the soft earth as though to prevent some invisible force from catching him up and tossing him off into space. All about was pitch darkness save for a few hangar lights on the far side of Singapore's R.A.F. Base. High overhead billions and billions of stars winked solemnly down on a world seemingly gone stark raving mad with war. In the distance there was sound, but it was so jumbled and so indistinct that it had no meaning for listening ears. For a brief instant Dave closed his eyes tight and pressed his face hard against the warm ground. Then he raised his head and turned it toward Freddy Farmer who hugged the ground right at his side.

"You're fully awake, aren't you, Freddy?" he whispered. "This wouldn't be any cockeyed nightmare I'm going through, would it?"

"A blasted fine chance of that!" the English youth replied with a groan. "I'm trying to make up my mind whether we're completely balmy, or just off our toppers. This is a mad business, Dave! Insane!"

"You're not telling me a thing!" Dawson breathed and squinted across the night blackened R.A.F. Base at the faint hangar lights. "But the heck of it is, we walked right into it, and we can't walk right out again!"

"If we could only get to the Raffles Hotel, and contact that agent of Bostworth's, and get some word to him!" Freddy Farmer said with a bitter sigh.

"I know," Dave grunted. "But Serrangi is no dummy no matter how you look at it. We haven't been out of his sight since we walked into the rug shop almost three hours ago. I had hoped he was going to let us come out here on our own. Maybe then we could have slipped by the Raffles and gotten some word to Bostworth. Nix, though! Serrangi came out with us in that Nineteen-Six jallopy, and showed us the path through the brush up to the edge of the field, here. And a funny sensation in the middle of my back tells me that he's back there a ways *still* keeping an eye on us. We sure picked something this time, pal. We picked a pip, and I ain't kidding."

"But if only Bostworth knew...!" Freddy began and let the rest trail off.

"Knew what?" Dave murmured. "That's the point! What could we really tell him that would make sense? Darn little, pal. Less than that, in fact. Serrangi tells us that at a given signal some rat at R.A.F. Base is going to blow lots of things sky high. He tells us that a Jap General has a hidden field with plenty planes up near Raja, in Burma. At the right time the Jap is going to blow the whistle, and things are supposed to pop in lots of places. And in my pocket I've got what looks like a pencil, only it's rolled up code data Serrangi gave us to give to General Kashomia. There you are."

"Well?" Freddy Farmer grunted. "Isn't that a lot?"

"It's nothing when you pick it apart," Dave said. "Figure it out. We don't know who the R.A.F. rat is, and Bostworth doesn't. Maybe there is a Jap general up at Raja with flocks of planes. So what? Is Bostworth going to send R.A.F. planes up there on our say-so to blast them out? Declare war on Japan, just like that? Fat chance! The British don't do things that way. Also, we don't know where the hidden field really is until we see the flare signals the Japs are to send up. Yeah! Burmese would get kind of sore if the British flew all over their country dumping bombs, trying to blast somebody they *think* is there. And here's a point, too. We don't know the striking date. It may be right after we get there ... and whether we get there, or not! Chances are, by the time Bostworth could induce Far East High Command to swing into action the Japs might be swinging their sneak haymaker. And this code data I've got in my pocket. Think Serrangi would have trusted us with it *if* there was even the slimmest chance that British Intelligence could break the code in time. Nuts! So what have we got?"

"You're right!" Freddy Farmer groaned. "Blasted little. Really nothing, when you come to look at it. But I hate to think of turning over that code data to General Kashomia! No doubt it's complete information of our strength, and such, here in the Far East. Probably high military secrets we've guarded for years."

"At least," Dave grunted. "And it puts us right behind the eight ball. We've *got* to turn it over to General Kashomia. Nothing happens until we do. And *we* can't do anything until something *does* happen. We've sort of got to pay out more rope, and pray we can take up the slack fast when we have to. If you get what I mean?"

"Yes, but what a chance we've got to take!" Freddy said in a voice that trembled slightly. "If we fail, Dave.... I mean, if things go through as the blasted Japs seem to be planning, the blood of Singapore will be on our hands. It will be because we failed. It...!"

Dave stuck out an elbow and jabbed the English youth in the side.

"Cut it!" he hissed. "That's not Freddy Farmer talking! Let's beat our brains out after we've failed. And, pal, that's something you and I just ain't going to up and do. Not while we can stand up and keep punching. So, heave that kind of talk in the river, Mister!"

Dave felt pressure on his arm, and heard Freddy's emotion choked voice.

"Thanks, Dave. I'm all right, now. I wish you'd kick me, and hard."

"I'll take a rain check on that invite," Dave said with a chuckle. "But forget it, Freddy. Heck! You'd up and leave me flat, if you knew some of the thoughts that have been breezing around in *my* head. So skip it. I guess it's this waiting that's getting us. I wish Serrangi's boys would hurry up and start the fireworks so's we can get started. You know, this sort of thing is darn near getting to be a habit."

"What is?" Freddy wanted to know.

"Posing as Axis agents, and swiping a British plane," Dave said. "Remember that time when we were on convoy patrol, and had to waltz off with that Catalina? We were plenty lucky then, and I've got a hunch we're going to have to be twice as lucky this time."[2]

"Lucky to get off without British bullets in our backs," Freddy Farmer murmured. "And lucky if *all* the gas tanks are filled. It will certainly be a blasted mess if our gas gives out and we have to force land somewhere in Thailand, or Burma."

Dave didn't make any reply to that for the simple reason there wasn't anything to be said. Perhaps the most pronounced fear of all regarding the wild, crazy venture into which they were plunging blindly was the fear of their fuel running out on them before they had reached the hidden airdrome in the wild Burmese mountains. If it was to be a Wellington or Whitley bomber they were to take aloft there wouldn't be any worry at all. But stealing a bomber was definitely out. It took time to get those babies off the ground, and possible British fighter planes giving chase could catch a bomber in short order. So it had to be the fastest two seater type at the Base. And as luck would have it they had spotted the six Bristol "Taurus" powered Fairey "Albacores" on the tarmac but a few seconds after they had reached the place where they now hugged the ground. They could make the distance in an Albacore. It might be close, but everything would be in their favor. They could get one off fast, they could gain altitude in the night sky fast, and an Albacore had a level flight speed that wasn't too much under the speed of a single seater fighter plane. Yes, it might be close, but an Albacore was their best bet. So they had picked the one they would rush for just as soon as Serrangi's men created the planned "disturbance" on the far side of the field.

But it was the body tingling waiting that dragged you down. It was like rats inside of you gnawing and gnawing at your nerves until you had to sink your teeth deep into your lips to stop from screaming and mentally flying apart in small pieces. Waiting! Waiting for what? A chance to rush out across the night shadowed drome, and smack into the withering fire of British guards? To steal a plane and race madly up into the night sky ... and be caught by British planes and sent hurtling earthward a ball of raging fire? To reach Raja and turn over the secret code data, and then stand by helpless as a gigantic, treacherous blow by the Nazi backed Japanese was struck at England in the Far East? To....

Dave shook his head savagely to blast the taunting thoughts from his brain. Many, many times in the past had he and Freddy tackled a problem that seemed hopeless, but never anything so seemingly utterly hopeless as this. It wasn't a case of just ferreting out the enemy's secret, and then smashing him. On the contrary, it was actually the direct opposite. Freddy and he were going to *give the enemy what he needed*, and then attempt to smash him *before he could make use of it*! Pure and simple, it was no more than handing a killer a loaded gun, and then taking it away from him before he could shoot you between the eyes. It was crazy, it was ridiculous, it was absurd, and it was insane. Yet it was the only thing they could do. They had to play it this way. There was no other loophole, and no chance to dive through it if one should suddenly present itself. It....

The rest of Dave's whirling thoughts spun off into oblivion as gun fire and wild shouting suddenly broke out on the far side of the field. It was like high voltage cutting through both of them, and they came up on their toes and fingertips as one man. For a brief instant they poised motionless eyes fixed on the tongue of flame that suddenly shot up from some building way over beyond the hangars. Then a silent signal passed between them and they went tearing bent well over out across one corner of the field toward the nearest Fairey Albacore some seventy yards away.

Seventy yards? It seemed seventy miles to Dave as he and Freddy Farmer fairly flew over the ground like a couple of frightened deer. With each racing step he took he half expected to see a British soldier rise right up out of the ground and level a rifle at him. No British soldier appeared, however, and hope zoomed in Dave as he saw the tarmac guards start running in the direction of the shouts, the shots, and the flames. The thought of death was not something that held him in fear and trembling. But to be mowed down by one of your own kind was a death no man would desire, if death it must be.

Seventy yards, thirty yards, ten yards, one yard! And then Dave and Freddy virtually vaulted into the pit of the Albacore. No plans had been made by them in advance about who would take what seat. It just happened to work out that Dave popped into the pilot's seat, and Freddy Farmer popped into the navigator-gunner's seat in back. Heart jammed up hard against his back teeth, and nervous sweat pouring off his body in rivers, Dave's fingers flew over the gas cocks, and starter, and ignition switches on the instrument panel. At the same time ... it was as though he had twenty hands instead of two ... he fastened the harness buckles of the seat parachute pack, hooked the safety belt clamp, opened up the throttle, and booted off the wheel brakes. The last operation was to jab the starter button ... and pray as he had never before prayed in all of his young years!

An eternity of heart crushing agony was Dave's, and then the Bristol Taurus in the nose roared up in its full throated song of power. The Albacore trembled and quivered for a brief instant and then shot forward as though ropes holding it back had been slashed through. Braced for the shock, Dave bent more forward over the stick and grimly waited for the craft to pick up sufficient take-off speed. With every revolution of the three-bladed steel propeller the plane tore faster and faster across the hard sun baked surface of the Base field. A thousand and one weird, crazy images seemed to pop up out of the ground just in front of the thundering plane. Dave's imagination went on a holiday during those few awful moments. He saw squads of British India troops loom up and blast away at the plane with rifle and machine gun fire, he saw armored cars rushing toward him from all angles, with guns blazing, and he saw a half division of tanks move like lightning into position to bar his way. He saw everything that an excitement quivering brain could conjure up. But all the plane actually crashed into was the air of night faintly tinted by the glow of the flames somewhere in back of the hangars.

And then the wheels lifted and Dave sent the Albacore curving up and around in the night sky. As he held the craft at its maximum climbing angle he twisted around in the seat and shot a quick glance down at the R.A.F. Base. Lights had sprung up all over the place, and he could just barely see the figures running toward the lines of planes. Some quarter of a mile in back of the row of hangars red flames were gutting an equipment stores building. The thing, however, that made Dave's heart slide down to its normal position in his chest was the utter absence of gun fire spitting up toward them. They had caught the field guards flat footed, and they would be well out of sight before British single seaters could come tearing up after them.

Taking his gaze off the scene below, Dave twisted all the way around and looked back at Freddy. In the pale light of the cockpit bulb the English youth's face was tense and set. And there was just a faint sadness in the eyes that stared down at the R.A.F. Base falling away from the Albacore's belly at a fast rate of speed.

"What's the matter, pal?" Dave called out. "Sad they didn't pepper away at us?"

"Don't talk rot!" Freddy snappily flinging him a scornful glance. "I'm jolly well tickled pink they didn't. I was just thinking that the Japs must never get Singapore, Dave. It means a lot to England, Singapore does. Like Gibraltar, and Malta."

"Oh, so that's all that's worrying you, huh?" Dave echoed. "I thought it was something serious. Well, go on back to sleep. I'll take care of everything for you, see?"

"That's splendid!" Freddy cracked and nodded downward. "As a starter, then, you can climb us a little faster. A couple of planes down there are taking off. And from here they look like Hawker Hurricanes!"

"Huh?" Dave yelled and shoved his head over the side. "My gosh, that's right. Hang on! I'm going to stick this baby right on her tail and go right up the pole!"

"Do that, and shut up!" Freddy said as the Bristol Taurus roared out in maximum power.

Holding the plane up as steeply as possible and toward the south Dave gave it his undivided attention until top service ceiling had been reached and the Island of Singapore was just another one of the blurred shadows thousands and thousands of feet below his wings. At top ceiling he leveled off and took a suck now and then on the oxygen tube he had stuck in his mouth to prevent sudden blacking out. Then on sudden impulse he killed the Albacore's engine and glided southward at a very flat angle while he spent the next five minutes scrutinizing the limitless expanse of night air behind and below. At the end of five minutes he started the engine again and heaved a little sigh of relief. They were clear of Singapore, and had succeeded in shaking off the two R.A.F. planes sent up to intercept them. Now, all that remained was to fly south for a spell, then double back up the middle of the South China Sea toward the southern tip of French Indo-China, and so on.

"Simple, in the bag!" Dave suddenly grated savagely as reaction set in. "All we have to do is the impossible. It should be a cinch!"

"What did you say, Dave?" came Freddy's voice.

"I said, I hope it'll be a nice day for something!" Dave grunted and shrugged his shoulders. "And do I *hope*!"

## CHAPTER THIRTEEN
### *Blue Water Rattlesnake*

Without warning the dawn sun came flaming up over the eastern lip of the wall, and as though the gods had thrown up millions and millions of invisible blinds, the shadows of night fled away into eternity and all was bathed in flashing gold light. For some time now, the Bristol powered Fairey Albacore had been prop clawing northward high above the endless rolling blue swells of the South China Sea. With the coming of the sun there had been a few seconds of wonder and nerve tingling strain for both Freddy and Dave. Although Freddy had plugged the radio into the Singapore wave length, and heard searching aircraft report they had lost all contact with the "stolen" plane, there was always the possibility that the "thieves" might find a flight or two of British aircraft right smack-dab in front of them when the new sun drove the night westward and out of sight.

However, as luck would have it, the exploding dawn light had found them completely alone in that section of the world's heavens. Both of them spent minutes staring hard in all directions. But there was nothing to see but the brassy blue sky above, and the brassy blue water below. Breathing a silent prayer in thanks of that small kindness, Dave turned around to Freddy.

"What's our position, Navigator?" he asked. "My rough figuring of wind, speed, and direction puts us almost within sight of land. Am I right or wrong, and what do those navigation gadgets back there tell you, huh?"

Freddy Farmer, in the act of bending over the plane's navigation instruments, lifted a hand for Dave not to bother him. Almost immediately he jerked up his head, though, pressed his fingertips to the built-in headphones of the helmet he wore, and stared straight ahead like a man suddenly sent into a trance. Dave opened his mouth to speak, but thought better of it. Obviously the English youth was getting something over the radio. And it was also obvious that he wasn't going to say anything about it until he had heard it all. And so instead of speaking, Dave bent down and began fiddling with the radio panel fitted to his own instrument panel. However, before he could shove in the radio-jack and tune the set Freddy Farmer was pounding him on the shoulder with one clenched fist, and yelling words in his ears.

"That was an SOS call to Singapore Base, Dave!" Freddy yelled. "It's a courier plane coming up from Australia. It's run into some kind of trouble. I couldn't tell what, because the message is all garbled up. But the operator says they are going down, and need help. I got their position signals just before they faded out. I figure that the spot is not over fifty miles to our east, Dave!"

"That's tough!" Dawson said and gave his pal a questioning look. "But what can we do about it, Freddy? This isn't a flyingboat. We couldn't sit down on the water and rescue them, even if we did find them."

"I know, I know!" Freddy said and gave a little shake of his head. "But, Dave.... But, Dave, it's possible that we're the only ones who got their signals. They were mighty weak. I almost missed them, myself. We could at least find the plane, and radio Singapore for them, and then get away before any R.A.F. Catalinas showed up."

Dave nodded slowly, but screwed up his face in a grimace of doubt and hesitation as he did so. True it was only fifty miles off their course. But that meant fifty miles off, and fifty miles back on again. A total of one hundred air miles. And they would be playing things close enough with the gas and oil supply, as it was. And, too....

"It's a British courier plane, and needs help, Dave!" Freddy Farmer's voice cut into his thoughts. "Blast it, we just can't let the lads down, Dave! We'd never be able to look each other in the face again, if we did."

Dave was forced to grin in spite of the seriousness of the situation. Good old Freddy Farmer. He was running true to form. His own neck was very, very far from being safe, and maybe he wouldn't even have a neck by this time tomorrow. Yet he wasn't giving that little item a single thought. Somebody else's life was in jeopardy, and that's all that concerned him at the moment. Help the other fellow, and then give a thought to himself ... maybe.

"Okay, okay!" Dave finally shouted and heeled the plane around on wingtip. "Did I say, no? Can't a guy argue, huh? But if we find out that they just thought they were being forced down then you're getting out and walking home, my little man. So here we go. And let's see you give those cat's eyes of yours a really good workout this time!"

A little over an hour later Dave dug knuckles into his tired, aching eyes, and once more looked down over the side of the Bristol Taurus powered Fairey Albacore, of the Singapore Fighter Command, at the seemingly endless expanse of the South China Sea. The burning rays of the brass ball, that was the sun hanging in the sky above, beat downward to turn the rolling swells into one great sheet of shimmering blue-green glass. To spot anything down there was like trying to spot a fly walking across the face of the sun, itself.

"Any luck, pal?" he called back over his shoulder to Freddy Farmer in the gunner's pit.

"No! And I think I'm going blind!" the English youth groaned. "That courier plane must have crashed in and sunk like a rock at once. This is the exact spot where they reported going down, but I swear there's nothing down there but water."

"And you're only looking at the *top* of it!" Dave grunted. "I wonder if we should chance calling Singapore Base, and...."

Dave cut himself off short and jerked his head around to the east. Perhaps it was just his imagination playing him tricks, but he could have sworn that he'd caught a strange flash of light out the corner of his eye that was more than just the rays of the burning sun bouncing up off the water. For a full minute, though, he peered intently at a point on the shimmering blue surface a good fifteen miles off his right wings. Then as he made a grimace of disappointment, and was about to turn his head front, he spotted it again. It was the sun's reflection on something that rose up out of the water and promptly fell back out of sight again.

"Hey, Eagle Eyes!" he called to Freddy Farmer and pointed a finger. "Take a look over there and down. Do you see what I see? And, if so, what in heck is it?"

It was several seconds before the English youth spoke, but when he did his voice trembled with excitement.

"That's the wing of a wrecked plane, Dave!" he cried. "Most of it's submerged ... maybe it's still attached to the plane ... but the swells are making it poke up out of water. It.... Dave! It has the R.A.F. bullseye on it. Must be the courier plane we've been hunting. Get us over there fast, Dave!"

The last was quite unnecessary. Dawson had already heeled the Albacore around on wingtip and was tearing full out in the direction of the strange looking object. And then, when they were still a few miles short of the spot, something else happened. Something that caused both youths to let out a simultaneous cry of wild excitement. The bow of a dull painted blue-green submarine came poking up through to the surface of the water not over a hundred yards from the bobbing wing.

In the matter of a few seconds the top half of the undersea craft was above water, and riding on an even keel. And once again Dave and Freddy saw the conning tower hatch open up, and squat little figures pop out and go scampering forward to the bow gun. It was the sight of that little bit of action that helped Freddy Farmer to find his tongue.

"That's the same boat as yesterday, Dave!" he cried. "Or an identical sister ship, anyway. Look out for the beggars. For heaven's sake don't let them shoot us down two days in a row. Better not get too close to the blighters."

Dave didn't say anything. The eyes he held fixed on the submarine were brittle with anger, and memory caused a lump of cold rage to swell up bigger and bigger inside of him. However, he made no effort to climb for altitude. As a matter of fact, he reached out his free hand and deliberately throttled the Bristol Taurus down to a whisper. Freddy reached forward and rapped him sharply on the shoulder.

"You in your right mind, Dave?" he cried. "What in the world's the idea? You're making us a perfect target for them. Have you gone balmy?"

"Not yet!" Dave barked and nosed the Albacore down into a long flat glide. "Shake up the old brains, pal. They don't see us, and can't. We're right in the sun to them. No! They're breaking out that bow gun for another purpose. And I've got a pretty good idea what it is, too."

"What?" Freddy demanded.

Dave nodded his head forward and down.

"To get rid of that plane wreckage that's bobbing around," he said. "Ask me and I'll tell you that the wreckage is all that's left of the courier plane that sent out that SOS. Remember our little unpleasant experience yesterday?"

"I'm jolly well not likely to forget it!" the English youth growled. "What about it?"

"I could be wrong, but I've got a hunch I'm not," Dave said with a deep scowl. "I mean it this way. This spot isn't far from where we spotted that strange sub yesterday throwing light signals at us. Well, we went down for a better look, and what happened? We got clipped before we had time to take a deep breath. Well, what happens to one guy can happen to somebody else. No law against it. See?"

"So far," Freddy grunted.

"Well, it's simple," Dave continued. "The courier plane was spotted by the sub. The sub, thinking it was Serrangi's R.A.F. boy friend, started flashing signals. Well, the courier plane boys went down to see what it was all about ... just like we did. And they caught just what we did ... only worse and more of it ... when the sub commander realized his mistake. The courier plane had time just to send the word to Singapore Base it was going down, and give its position, before it crashed in. Well, the sub heard those signals and after ducking away, came back to remove all traces of their dirty work. And.... And that's what they're doing right now!"

Dave shouted the last as the two bow guns aboard the submarine belched out flame and smoke and hurled a couple of shells at the bobbing wing at almost blank range. At practically the same instant there were two white splashes of water not a yard from the bobbing wing. And then a great column of frothy foam and billowing smoke towered upward into the air. And for a brief instant the sun drenched blue water seemed to split apart and spew up a mess of tangled water-logged wreckage. Just a split second look at the shattered wreckage was all that the boys were allowed before froth and boiling foam sucked the mess down out of sight forever. But that split second was long enough for them both to see that the wreckage had once been an R.A.F. long range Consolidated Catalina flyingboat. The type that is used all over the world by the British for courier plane work.

"That was the courier plane, right enough!" Freddy Farmer said in a choked voice. "Blast their dirty souls. They shot the poor devils down in cold blood, like they tried to do to us. And, now ... and now, they...."

The English youth couldn't go on, he was so choked up with blind rage. A split instant later Dave opened up his engine wide and stuck the Albacore's nose down in a wing screaming dive.

"Man those rear guns, Freddy!" he thundered at the top of his voice. "Maybe England hasn't declared war on Japan, but you and I are declaring war on that stinking Jap pig-boat down there ... and right now!"

"But we've no depth bombs, or torpedo!" Freddy cried, but nevertheless swiveling around and unlocked his rear guns.

"Who cares?" Dave roared and hunched forward over the stick. "There's a few of those brown rats on deck. We can at least cook their goose. We.... Hold your hat! They've sighted us, and are trying to bring their guns to bear. No, you don't ... you dime a dozen, slant eye bums!"

As Dave snarled the last he flipped off the guard cap of the electric trigger button of his forward guns, and jabbed the button home. His guns yammered out a savage song of death and the group of little brown figures clustered about the forward guns seem to melt to the deck and roll off into the water, before either of the two guns could spew its load of destructive shrapnel upward.

However, no sooner did the bow gunners take their dose of death and spill into the water than a new crew popped up out of the conning tower hatch and scurried forward to replace them. Others also popped up into view, each armed with a portable machine gun. They dropped in back of the conning tower bridge for what protection it would afford them and began blazing away. Dave felt the Albacore shake and tremble a little as a well placed burst went tearing up through the right wings. But he didn't swerve from his straight downward plunge a hair. He and Freddy would have to risk the machine gun fire. It was the bow guns he had to put out of action. Rather, he had to send the second crew spilling off after the first. Let those two guns get in their licks and the Albacore would be a mess of metal toothpicks flying about in the air.

And so Dave held the plane steady and tore down until it looked as though he were going to dive right into the bow mounted guns. In the last instant allowed he let fly with his guns, practically tore the new gun crews to bleeding shreds with his deadly fire, and went curving upward and around to give Freddy Farmer a point blank shot at the half crouching machine gunners. And the English youth didn't waste a split second, or a single shot from his twin guns. His fire was every bit as deadly as Dave's, and it knocked over the crouching machine gunners like a shotgun would knock over frozen birds perched on an icy telephone wire. The little Japs went down like ten pins. And what's more, they stayed down!

Then, suddenly, as Freddy Farmer let drive with a parting burst, a column of orange red flame came shooting up out of the open conning tower. It leaped three hundred feet straight up into the air and then blossomed out on all sides like a gigantic flower of fire. At almost the same instant invisible giants down in the depths of the shimmering blue water seemed to push upward against the keel of the submarine. The whole craft rose clear out of water, seemed to hover motionless for a split second, and then buckle in the middle and fall back in again. White spray, red flame, and boiling smoke spread out in all directions. And then presently there was nothing but an ever widening oil slick on the water to indicate the spot where the submarine had gone down for good.

Struck speechless by the weird, horrible sight, both boys stared frozen eyed for a long moment. Then Dave shook himself out of his trance and hauled the Albacore off the top of its zoom. Once the plane was level he twisted around and grinned at Freddy.

"What was that about not having depth bombs, or aerial torpedoes?" he echoed. "Boy! With you around to shoot right down the open conning tower and touch off something in her innards, we don't need anything else. Nice going, pal! That gets you a kewpie doll, or something."

"Think *what* it gets me, if British High Command ever finds out!" Freddy Farmer said in a tight voice. "Good Lord, Dave! I've just sunk a Japanese submarine, and...."

"Yeah, I know!" Dave cut in sharply. "England's not even at war with Japan ... yet! The big shots in London and Tokio haven't made it official, yet. Lot of good that did *us* yesterday, didn't it! And a lot of good it did those poor devils aboard the courier plane! Nuts! You and your traditional rules of war give me a pain in the neck. Wake up, little man. That sort of thing is all changed these days. Nowadays you hit first, you hit hard, and you hit for keeps! If you don't you're going to find yourselves waking up in a hospital ... if you *do* wake up!"

"Yes," Freddy Farmer mumbled and swallowed hard. "Yes, of course you're dead right. But, it gives a chap a queer feeling just the same. I mean, if that had been a Nazi U-boat, why...."

"Who says a Nazi wasn't her commander?" Dave snapped. "Jap, Nazi, or one of Mussolini's funny looking things! Who cares? It's down where it belongs, now. And down to stay. And I still say that was sweet shooting, sonny boy. Sinks a sub with a couple of machine guns. No, I guess we'd better not ever report it. Nobody would ever believe us. We'd be called a couple of first class.... *Omigosh!*"

"What's the matter?" Freddy Farmer cried in alarm as Dave stiffened and jerked his head front. "Another one?"

"No such luck!" Dave cried and heeled the Albacore around toward the northwest. "I'll have to wait until next time for my chance to duplicate your neat little trick. No. I just took a look at the gas gauges? Did you ever do much camping out, Freddy? I mean, just go out and live off the land, and all that sort of thing?"

"I have a little," Freddy replied. Then sharply, "But what the blasted blazes are you raving about, now? What *is* the matter?"

"Not a thing, not a thing!" Dave chanted and stuck the nose down slightly to pick up all the extra speed he could. "Only we've been using up fuel like there was a filling station out here every other mile. Unless Lady Luck gives us one awful big break we may have to do some camping out tonight somewhere maybe in the wilds of Thailand or Burma."

"But we can't, Dave!" Freddy cried before he could check his tongue. "We've got to get to Raja, or ... or Lord knows what may happen."

Dave turned around and squinted an eye at his pal.

"Brother, are you kidding?" he muttered. "Or didn't you think I knew that?"

---

## CHAPTER FOURTEEN
### *Raja, the Invisible*

---

For the ten millionth time in the last five minutes Dave Dawson let his eyes come to rest on the main and emergency gas tank gauges on the instrument board. Both needles were pressed hard against the zero peg, and they had been that way for the last five minutes. It was as though the powerful engine in the nose was now simply running on its reputation. Of course, that wasn't true. Even when the gauge shows you have no gas there is always a certain amount left in the feed lines that will permit the power plant to function for a bit longer. But the Bristol Taurus had been turning over for five full minutes on seemingly dry tanks, and as far as Dave was concerned that was most certainly some kind of a record for aircraft engines.

And so as he stared at the gauges again there was bewildered amazement in his eyes ... and a cold lump of fear in his stomach. If Freddy's navigation had been accurate, and if the land marks they had been able to sight from their high altitude really were those that were marked on the flight map Serrangi had given them, they were still a good fifty or sixty miles short of their destination!

If they were flying over England, or the States, or eastern Canada, or places like that, there would be no cause for worry and the cold lump of fear. But, they were flying over the godawful region of the world cut by the Thailand-Burma border. And they had only to glance down over the side to realize full well what would happen when their engine finally gave up and they were forced down. True, they might live through it; they stood a chance. Perhaps it was only a million to one chance. However, if they could sit down in the tree tops, or on the side of the rocky jagged peaked mountains, or on the bottom of some jungle choked gorge ... and not break every bone in their bodies ... everything would be fine. At least for the time being. What happened tomorrow, the next week, and the next year, were things best not to think about.

"We've got to make it, Dave! We've got to make it! Get all the altitude you can. It will give us a longer glide."

Dave clenched his teeth hard, and fought back the savage impulse to spin around and let fly with a barrage of verbal abuse at Freddy Farmer. Only the cold realization that his own pal's nerves were every bit as frayed as his prevented him from doing so. And after all, for the last hour it had been Freddy Farmer who had kept the conversation going to take their thoughts off the approaching inevitable, and ease the torturing strain somewhat. Yes, they had to make it. But would they? If the engine should cut out now would they be able to make the rest of the distance in a glide? True, they had almost top ceiling under their wings, but it would still be a long glide. And to reach the spot indicated on the map and then circle it five times at the exact altitude of six thousand feet was something that was strictly up to the gods. In his heart, Dave had the quaking feeling that they wouldn't be able to circle the spot once at even six feet.

"Or even reach it!" he spoke the thought harshly. "We got us a Jap sub, but heaven knows what wasting that time is going to cost us."

"And it was my fault, Dave!" Freddy Farmer's voice suddenly spoke in Dave's ear. "I'm sorry as can be. I shouldn't have suggested that we go look for the courier plane. After all, we were on a mighty important mission."

Dave swung around and fixed him with a scornful eye.

"Eavesdropping on what a guy even says to himself, huh?" he growled. Then softening his words with a grin, "You stick to your knitting, son, and leave us grown-ups alone. And don't start grabbing off credit for going on that courier plane hunt. I had my mind all made up to do it before you so much as opened your yap. I was just waiting to hear what you thought of the idea. And besides, this little old engine hasn't stopped *yet*, has it?"

The last word hadn't even started to become an echo before the Bristol Taurus in the nose uttered a few rusty metallic gasps and then became silent as a tomb, save for the soft swish of the propeller as momentum turned it over in the wind. Freddy Farmer gulped and forced a smile to his lips.

"Yes, I'm afraid it has, Dave," he said. "But it's certainly been a blasted wonder up to now. Well, we've got lots and lots of altitude for gliding. And now that the engine's stopped, it is a bit peaceful up here, don't you think?"

"Very," Dave said with a nod. Then chuckling, "I'd like to stay up here awhile. Boy! *How* I'd like to stay up here awhile! But I always was a selfish cuss. Any particular altitude at which you'd like to get out, Mister? We're making all stops on the way down, you know."

"Just let me out at the ground floor!" Freddy replied with a slight grin on his stiff lips. "And I mean the ground floor, not the basement, my good man!"

Dave gave a little wave of his hand to acknowledge the wisecrack and then concentrated every ounce of his attention on keeping the Fairey Albacore just a hair below the stalling point. Every inch of altitude he saved was at least five inches farther forward the plane would be able to travel. It wasn't a question of precious feet, or yards, or miles, now. It was a matter of inches. And every additional inch was just another little bit in their favor.

But as Dave held the controls in a steel fingered grip and peered narrow eyed ahead at the heart chilling terrain, the little hammers of dread and doubt began to pound away in his brain. His mouth and throat became dry, and the cold lump of lead formed once more in the pit of his stomach. He had flown over a lot of terrible country in his time, but nothing like this. As far as he could see in any direction there wasn't a piece of flat ground big enough to place your foot on. Nothing but jagged rock sided mountains, and deep ravines choked with jungle growth. A plane force-landing would be ripped to ribbons before it touched the ground. And even though its occupants did live through the crash it would really be only postponing death. Death in a thousand different forms would be waiting for them down there in the jungle when they tried to fight their way out to civilization. It was an airman's graveyard, that's what it was. It....

Dave cut short the rest of his disagreeable thoughts as he felt Freddy Farmer's hand pound down on his shoulder, and heard the English youth's excited voice in his ears.

"Bear a few degrees to port, Dave!" Freddy cried. "I guess our compass must have gone a bit balmy, or my last calculation of position was wrong. Look way over there to the left and ahead! There's the sharp S bend in the Salween River that's marked on this map. Dave! If I'm right, we're not in the soup at all. We should make that easily in a glide. And not get down below six thousand feet, either!"

Dave leaned forward, wiped the back of his hand across his stinging eyes, and squinted hard. But the hope that had zoomed up within him at Freddy Farmer's words took a nose dive when he couldn't see anything on the ground that looked like the S turn in a river. As far as he could see the few square miles indicated by Freddy's pointed finger weren't one bit different from the hundreds of other square miles of treacherous terrain he could see. However, hope didn't die completely within him because this was not the first time Freddy's eagle sharp eyes had spotted things long before he had.

Just the same after nosing the plane to port a bit and slushing forward at the flat gliding angle, the tiny flame of hope burned lower and lower.

"Don't you see it, Dave?" Freddy called out finally.

"Not yet!" Dave replied grimly. "And I hope it's not a mirage you're seeing. But.... Hold everything! Yeah! see it now, Freddy. Gee! It looks exactly like a curving shadow on the jungle trees. Yes, that's the S bend. And we'll make it easy, Freddy, easy. Remind me to hang another medal on you for sweet eyesight. Me, I would have glided right on by and not known the difference. Okay, boy! Looks like we're coming to the end of the line."

"And the beginning of the worst part, I fancy," Freddy Farmer muttered through clenched teeth. "Lord, Dave! I hope that beggar, Serrangi, told us the truth. I mean, that there really is a hidden drome down there."

"Me, too, and how!" Dave echoed almost reverently. "Between you, me, and that dead engine in the nose, I'd be tickled pink to drop right down into Uncle Goering's arms right about now. But, sweet tripe, Freddy! How could there possibly be a secret drome down there? A hole in one of the mountains, perhaps? And they shoot them off by catapult? It just doesn't seem possible, so help me!"

"It's got to be, it's got to be!" the English youth repeated over and over. "If we've come this far just to land in some blasted trees, I'll ... I'll never forgive that black hearted blighter, Serrangi, as long as I live!"

Freddy Farmer's crazy remark snapped the tension a little and caused Dave to laugh out loud.

"That's telling him, Freddy, old sock!" he cried. "Boy! Would Serrangi be sore if you never forgave him!"

"Go ahead and laugh!" Freddy snapped. "But we're not out of the woods, yet!"

"Oh, yes, we are!" Dave corrected. "And what we want to do is *stay out* of them and not *get in* them. Catch on?"

"Quite!" Freddy snapped again. Then thrusting his hand over Dave's shoulder, he cried, "And there's something else very funny, my lad. The altimeter. We've got not over four thousand feet left before we reach the altitude when we start our circle signals."

"Sure, I know," Dave said good naturedly. "Keep your pants on. Little Dave has everything under control ... he hopes. Yup! We make it easy. Get your eyes skinned, Freddy, for signals. We're going to be over the spot almost any instant, now."

It was, perhaps, four full minutes before Dave brought the Albacore directly over the middle of the S bend in the river, and at an altitude just a shade over six thousand feet. He had allowed an extra hundred feet so that he would not go too far below the six thousand foot mark by the time he had completed his five circles. After all, Serrangi had been most particular about sticking at six thousand feet. And for that reason he couldn't take chances. If there were Jap guns down there trained on the Albacore....

Dave swallowed hard, shook himself as though to drive off the unpleasant possibility, and hauled the Albacore around for the first circle. He guided the plane by instinct, keeping the nose no higher than the law of gravity would allow. He stuck his head out through the opened cockpit hatch and stared intently downward. Freddy Farmer was doing the same thing, and like two men of stone they sat rigid in the pit, not speaking, and hardly daring to breathe.

Three, four, and five times Dave completed a circle, and by his expert flying the plane didn't lose more than a hundred feet. The altimeter needle quivered at the six thousand foot peg when he came out of the final circle and glided straight northward. That also he did by instinct for his eyes were still riveted to the ground below. Perhaps ten seconds clicked by, or perhaps it was ten years. But, suddenly, a red ball of fire seemed to zoom right up out of the lush green jungle below them and come arcing up toward the belly of their plane. It mounted upward no more than a couple of hundred feet, probably, then curved over and down to wink out before it struck ground.

"The signal flare, Dave!" Freddy Farmer roared at the top of his voice. "Serrangi didn't lie to us! There is somebody down there."

"I knew it all the time, I did!" Dave cracked back, as his heart looped in his chest with joy. "But, I still want to know *where* in heck a field could be down there. It's.... Holy smoke! Am I seeing things, or ... or what?"

Dave stuttered out the rest as he stared in dumbfounded amazement down toward earth. An airplane had suddenly appeared before his very eyes. It was a swift Japanese Nakajima 96 single seater. A Land of the Rising Sun copy of the American Boeing F4B. But the cockeyed point was that the craft, with its red and white rising sun markings and all, had seemingly popped right out of a tree top. One instant Dave had been staring at the top of the lush jungle stretch below him, and in the next he was looking at a Jap plane zooming up toward him at top climbing speed. It was incredible, it was nuts, and it was all cockeyed. But, nevertheless, it was fact. The Jap plane was coming up like a rocket off on a holiday.

"Dave! I'm not crazy, am I?" came Freddy Farmer's tight voice. "That is a Jap plane, isn't it?"

"Unless we're both crazy!" Dave replied and watched the Jap pilot swing out wide of them, and then curve back in toward their right wings. "But where in thunder he came from, don't ask, pal, don't ask! Jumping Messerschmitts! Will we have something to tell the boys ... if we ever get back!"

"You could have left off that last bit," Freddy grunted. "I don't want to even think about that. There! The lad is signalling, Dave! He's motioning for us to swing in behind him, and follow him down."

"Yeah!" Dave said with a nod. "This time I see it with my own eyes. That dirty brown rat! Boy, is it a temptation, Freddy!"

"What do you mean?" the English born R.A.F. ace demanded.

"That Jap," Dave said and went through the motion of depressing the electric trigger button on the stick. "Could I shoot the buck teeth out of him from here! And with both eyes shut, too! I...."

"Dave, don't be mad!" Freddy cried in alarm. "That would be a fine mess."

"Don't be dumb!" Dave shut him up and chuckled. "Do you think I am? I was only *thinking* how good it would make me feel, that's all. Well, here we really start down, and from now on it's going to be miracles, as far as I'm concerned. They say a Jap is as good as a monkey in a tree. Maybe they've got planes that cling to branches like monkeys too. But, if so, it's going to be too bad for this baby *we're* in!"

What happened in the next five minutes was actually not a series of miracles being revealed for the benefit of the thumping hearted and aching eyed R.A.F. aces in the Albacore. However, it might just as well have been. The nearer they glided to the earth in the wake of the Jap plane, the more and more they both became convinced that there wasn't a spot big enough for a fly to sit down in down there. However, when no more than eight hundred feet separated the belly of their plane from the ground the big "miracle" came to pass.

Actually, it was simply the truth registering in their amazement filled eyes. It was not all lush jungle down there. No, not all. They suddenly saw a half mile long, and two hundred foot wide strip of jungle that wasn't jungle at all. It only*looked* like jungle. It was a cleared off section of ground with camouflage covering so cleverly painted that it all blended in perfectly with the surrounding lush green, rock studded landscape. The "strip" ran straight along the lip of a deep ravine, so that if there seemed to be any difference where the camouflage met the real thing, it would be taken as a line where the edge of the ravine dropped off.

Almost not daring to believe his eyes, Dave gingerly worked the Albacore around and down toward the southern end of the camouflage strip. The Jap plane was little more than a couple of hundred yards in front of him. And even as Dave turned the Albacore around on a line with the long side of the camouflage strip, the Jap plane touched earth and quickly taxied ahead until it virtually disappeared under the heavy jungle foliage at the far end.

Another fifteen seconds, or so, and Dave's wheels touched ground. For reasons of personal safety, and also to impress eyes that were unquestionably watching he made a sweet feather-on-velvet landing and let the plane truddle slowly forward to finally come to a full stop. But, no sooner had he stopped rolling than half a dozen Jap mechanics dashed out, and grabbed the wing tips, and motioned for him to taxi ahead. He shook his head, and pointed to the dead engine. One of the mechanics, who seemed to be in charge, turned his head and shrilled something toward the jungle growth in his native tongue. In practically nothing flat a dolly crew came streaking out. And in just about the same time the other mechanics hoisted up the tail of the Albacore, and the dolly was run under it. Chattering like magpies they caught hold of the dolly handle and dragged Dave and Freddy backwards off the camouflage strip and in under the shelter of the jungle trees. To Dave it was like being hauled backwards into the yawning entrance of a tunnel. One moment the brassy sun was glaring down on him, and in the next he was in semi-darkness and staring out through an opening at the sun flooded world.

# CHAPTER FIFTEEN
## *Sons of Nippon*

The faint jar as the Albacore's tail was lifted out of the dolly trough and lowered none too gently to the ground, seemed to snap Dave out of his trance. He licked his lips, swallowed hard and took a good look around. For a few seconds he didn't see anything but blurs because of the sudden change of light. But when they did focus and the blurs took on definite shapes and outlines, he came within a hair's breadth of letting out a wild yell of amazement. Even at that he did start violently, and his eyes popped out of their sockets like marbles on sticks.

What he saw was perhaps the most weird, grotesque, unbelievable sight he had ever seen since the day of his birth. True, he had seen the underground airdromes and hangars the Nazis had constructed along the Franco-German border, and he had seen the expertly camouflaged fields built by the German Luftwaffe on the burning sands of the Libyan desert. But this hidden field and array of nature made hangars were almost beyond the powers of even one's wildest imaginations. On three sides of him were row after row of Japanese military planes. They were of all types from the small Nakajima that had come up to lead him down to the giant long range Mitsubishi bombers. They were parked wing to wing, with a small plane between each two big ones, so that there didn't have to be any reshifting around when the time came for them to take off. One by one they would go shooting down the jungle tunnel to flat open ground, and then up into the air ... like a string of beads coming undone, or a row of stitches being pulled put.

But there was much more to the scene than just the row after row of parked planes. Much more. Included also was all the mobile equipment needed to service the craft, and keep them in constant perfect condition. There were also great piles of bombs, and small mountains of cans filled with high test gas and oil. There were jungle huts used for living quarters. Huts where meals were obtained. In a few words, that area of the Burma jungle covered an entire active service airdrome complete from cook stoves to death dealing winged chariots of war.

"*Gott!* Once I leave here I shall never believe that I have seen such a thing!"

The voice was that of Freddy Farmer speaking in German. It was a tip to Dave to remember the part he played, but it was also a truly felt belief of the English youth. He had slipped out of his 'chute and safety belt harness, and was standing up in his pit and looking around out of eyes that had widened as large as dinner plates.

"And I agree with you, my comrade!" Dave exclaimed hastily in the same tongue to let Freddy know he was on his guard. "I can hardly wait to tell *Der Fuehrer* what a wonderful thing we have seen with our own eyes. It is indeed a great tribute to the cleverness of our brave and loyal allies!"

As Dave spoke the words he looked down at the group of buck toothed, wide grinning brown faces about the plane. Instinct told him that a couple of them understood German, but he acted as though he believed it an unknown foreign tongue to them.

"We come from Serrangi, of Singapore!" he boomed out. "It is to be our great honor to report to General Kashomia. Does one of you speak German, and can escort us to his exalted presence?"

A squat, chunky Jap, who make Dave think of a fire hydrant with a face, pushed close to the side of the plane, beamed and bobbed his shaven head up and down.

"Whoever comes from Serrangi, is always expected," the man said in perfect German. "Permit me to introduce myself. I am Captain Kito. It will be my honor to escort you to where General Kashomia waits. Will you be so pleased as to descend from your plane?"

It wasn't until he had climbed down and was facing the Jap that Dave realized the man carried a helmet and goggles in his hand. Undoubtedly the man was the pilot of the pursuit plane that had come up to lead him down. The little Jap stood stiff as a post, then bowed from the waist at the two new arrivals like a mechanical doll. Then, whirling, he spat out something at the others grouped about. They instantly split and fell back to form a pathway. The Jap looked back at Dave and Freddy and showed his buck teeth in a broad smile, then started forward rapidly for all the world like a little brown terrier on the end of a leash.

The way led past the rows of planes, and stores of fuel and bombs, to the jungle huts on the far side. There was a clearing in front of the huts and several Japanese pilots were lounging about, taking things easy. They flashed quick glances at Dave and Freddy, but what they saw apparently didn't interest them much, for they all immediately resumed whatever they were doing. Perhaps visitors to this secret airdrome were common to them. Or perhaps it was part of their training to show no interest in anything save the knifing of a man in the back. Preferably one who had been their friend!

The squat Jap pilot finally came to a stop in front of the largest of the huts. It was constructed mostly of bamboo, and on stilts that allowed a three foot clearance between the floor and the soft spongy ground. Evidently General Kashomia was taking no chances with crawling jungle things, human or otherwise! The Jap paused before the hut, bowed reverently before it, then turned to Dave and Freddy.

"If you will please be so good as to ascend," he said, and gestured with his hand at the little bamboo ladder. "I will go and order that food and drink be prepared for you when you have completed your business with General Kashomia."

With a parting bob of his head the Jap pilot pivoted about and went off at his restless gait. Dave grinned at Freddy, then shrugged and started up the ladder. A few seconds later he was standing on solid plank flooring and facing three men who sat cross legged Japanese style about a table that wasn't over eighteen inches off the floor. Three pairs of brownish-black eyes stared at him expressionlessly, and unwaveringly. In an odd sort of way he was reminded of the nerve rasping moments when he and Freddy had first entered Serrangi's room in the Devil's Den. If there was any difference it was that the eyes of these three dressed in the battle uniforms of high ranking Japanese air force officers showed even less expression than had Serrangi's hypnotic eyes. The same hunch came to Dave that had come to him in Serrangi's place. He went ramrod stiff and flung up his right arm, fingers extended stiff and close together.

"*Heil Hitler!*" he shouted.

"*Heil Hitler!*" Freddy Farmer at his side echoed, only louder.

The Jap officer seated in the middle inclined his head slightly and made a little motion with one hand that was probably an acknowledgment of the greeting. There was nothing particularly military about it, however. Nor respectful, for that matter, and Dave had the sneaky feeling that the name of Adolf Hitler didn't cut such a terrible lot of ice with the Japs in this part of the world. They had business of their own to attend to that was thousands of miles removed from Berlin. Also, of late the Nazis were getting belted all over the place by the hard hitting Russians. They had come within thirty miles of Moscow to be stopped cold, and Hitler's boast to spend Christmas in the Kremlin was fast going right out the window.

"We come from Serrangi in Singapore," Dave finally said when the three Japs just continued to stare at them. "We come to give something to General Kashomia. You are General Kashomia?"

Dave looked questioningly at the middle Jap, and the man inclined his head again.

"I am General Kashomia," he said in flawless Berlin German, and extended a bony hand. "Give to me what you bring from Serrangi in Singapore."

A tiny almost indistinguishable spark of light had flickered up in the son of Nippon's eyes. But apart from that he gave the impression that he was no more interested in what Dave handed to him than he would be in last week's newspaper. He took the tight roll of paper that looked like a pencil and without a word handed it to the officer on his right. That man took a knife from his belt and deftly slit the outer wrapping its entire length and smoothed out flat the five or six sheets contained inside. As though he had peeled and prepared an orange for his master he handed the lot back to General Kashomia.

The high ranker accepted it just as blank faced and nonchalant as before. Then with a quick stiffening of his legs he rose up onto his feet.

"I will learn what Serrangi has to tell me," he said, and waved for Dave and Freddy to squat down. "Be seated and rest yourselves after your long journey. A *very* long journey for the type of plane you flew."

Brown black eyes bored into Dave's as General Kashomia spoke the last. Then the Jap turned quickly and disappeared through a bamboo laced door at the rear. Dave and Freddy squatted down, looked at each other for a brief instant, and then gave their attention to the two remaining Jap officers. It was like giving their attention to the stone lions in front of the New York Public Library. The two Japs just squatted there and stared off into space as though nothing else existed. Dave stood the nerve racking silence for a moment, and then broke it.

"Doesn't your honored General Kashomia believe we come from Singapore?" he asked harshly.

Brown black eyes pivoted around in heavy lidded sockets to focus on him, but neither Jap uttered a sound. Presently one of them was apparently struck with the bright idea of hand signals. He pointed at Dave's mouth, then at his own ears, and shrugged to indicate he neither spoke nor understood the German tongue. Dave relaxed, then almost jumped up straight in the air as Freddy Farmer whispered hoarsely in his ear.

"The swine probably lies!" he said. "I'm sure he speaks our German tongue as well as we do. Yes! You and I will have much to report when we return to Berlin."

For a brief instant Dave thought that Freddy had gone nuts, but when he noticed that neither of the Japs so much as batted an eye, and caught Freddy Farmer's faint sigh of relief, he realized that the words had been spoken to catch the Japs off guard. To insult them and see whether they did understand German or not. But evidently they didn't for Freddy's swine insult sailed right over their shaven heads.

"Take it easy!" Dave breathed at Freddy. "The one in the next room understands us, you know. I don't feel very much like having my throat cut today. Don't get too smart with these fellows. They may be tough, too."

"I won't," the English youth grunted. "But all that business out there. It's unbelievable! It makes your blood run cold."

"Not mine," Dave murmured. "It was frozen stiff before we started. But.... Oh-oh!"

The bamboo laced door swung open and General Kashomia reappeared. He was as blank faced as ever save for two dull reddish spots of excitement on his cheeks. His step was quicker, too, and there was a ring in whatever he sing-songed at his two lesser ranks. They turned to him at once, their eyes lighted up, and they both vigorously bobbed their heads up and down and seemed to chant sounds of their native tongue. General Kashomia answered them, and they shut up. Then the senior officer squatted down in the middle and fixed his eyes on the two R.A.F. aces.

"My humble apologies for even thinking you could have come from elsewhere but Serrangi in Singapore," he said. "And the highest praise from myself and all my countrymen for so spectacular a flight. It is one I should not like to do in anything but a large plane. You are indeed a credit to the Luftwaffe."

"It was a small undertaking," Dave said with a boastful shrug. "Most any pilot and navigator in the Luftwaffe could have made it. I understand, then, that we have brought you good news, yes?"

The Jap general's lids contracted slightly, and the tiny gleam leaped into his eyes again.

"Serrangi always sends one good news," he said slowly. "That is why he is a wealthy man. There is one part that is not clear, however. The new location of Singapore Island's water supply. There has been a second underground reservoir constructed near Mandai?"

If it was a trick question meant to trap the boys, it fell flatter than yesterday's pancakes. Both Dave and Freddy shook their heads. And it was Freddy who answered the question ... truthfully.

"We know almost nothing of Singapore, General Kashomia," he said. "We have spent but one day and a night in the Singapore area. The good news that Serrangi gives to you, he did not give to us. It was but by a bit of good fortune that we were able to act as couriers."

If that news surprised General Kashomia he did not show it. However, his next words indicated that he wasn't getting all of the picture, yet.

"Strangers to Singapore?" he murmured. Then, "But not of course to Serrangi?"

"Yes!" Dave shot right back at him and got a little comfort and satisfaction out of the shadow of annoyed bewilderment that passed over the Jap's face.

"That is interesting," the son of Nippon said presently. "You will be good enough to explain, please? You are strangers to Singapore, and to Serrangi, also? Yet you fly here to where I wait, and place the means of a great military triumph in my hands? I have spent much time in Berlin, but I am afraid I shall never fully understand you Germans. The words you speak confuse me."

For a crazy second Dave was tempted to give the Jap a cockeyed story that would practically set him on his ear with perplexity. On second thought, though, he killed the urge. And for two very good reasons. One was because the Jap might have some means of checking his words, and, considering their immediate situation, it might not go so well for Freddy and himself to be caught in a lie. The second reason was because his eyes had become completely accustomed to the interior of the hut on stilts, and he was able to see the array of military maps hung on the walls. They included all sections of that part of the world, and although the Japanese paint brush notations meant nothing to him, a series of lines and arrows drawn on the maps had started his heart thumping against his ribs with suppressed excitement. Unless he was all wrong the maps definitely proved that here at Raja was the center of a Japanese spider's web of death and intrigue that reached far out in all directions.

And so Dave settled himself a bit more comfortably and told General Kashomia the same story he had told Serrangi. The Jap listened in stony faced silence right through to the end. When Dave finished he asked a few pointed questions, and appeared satisfied with the answers the two R.A.F. aces gave him. However, not because the blank expression on his face altered any. Simply because he shrugged and stopped asking questions.

"We Japanese have long admired your great Luftwaffe," the little brown son of Nippon finally said. "As you probably know, there have been Luftwaffe instructors in Japan for many years. They have taught us much, and the hour fast approaches when we shall prove we were good pupils. Yes, the news you bring me from Serrangi, in Singapore, makes our great hour approach at great speed."

The blank, inscrutable face lighted up with a seething inner flame for a brief instant, and the Jap's brown black eyes slid around to glance quickly at the array of maps. A pointed question hovered on the tip of Dave's lips, but before he could get it off Freddy Farmer spoke up.

"As we left Serrangi," the English youth said gravely, "there was mention of a request you might be so good as to grant us."

"Request?" the Jap echoed in a hissing voice, as his eyes fairly snapped around to Freddy's face. "Then you did make that wonderful flight ... for a price?"

It was a wonderful opening for a bit of play acting by Freddy, and the English youth was quick to take full advantage of the opportunity. He puffed out his chest, pulled in his chin, and glared at the Jap general.

"Everything we do, we do only for the great love we have for our Fuehrer, and our Fatherland!" he shouted. "The request that might be made has to do only with further service we might give to our glorious mutual cause."

"I humble myself before you," the Jap murmured and bowed low. "Your first words watered the seed of a different thought within me. I was mistaken. This request. What is it then?"

"Between his words," Freddy said slowly as the pounding of his own heart kept time with Dave's, "Serrangi hinted of great disaster to befall the British in Singapore. He whispered the suggestion that we beg of you the honor of taking part in the delivery of this great blow. His hints told us plainly that it would be a sight we would remember to our graves. Our Fuehrer has taught us to always be a soldier, and to always obey orders. We are here in Raja, so we are your soldiers, and your orders are orders we would obey even as though they came from the lips of our own Fuehrer. If you so order, we will not move one step from Raja. But it is my dearest wish, and that of my famous Luftwaffe comrade, here, that you do not give such an order. We pray and hope that our eyes, our hands, and our bodies may help you avenge at Singapore the Luftwaffe losses against the British Royal Air Force last winter. We took part in that air battle against the English and it would put joy in our hearts if you would permit us to help take the lives of ten British at Singapore for every one of our Luftwaffe friends we with our own eyes saw fall over Britain."

The speech was one of the best Dave had ever heard drop from Freddy Farmer's lips, and it was all he could do to look pleadingly at General Kashomia, and not leap to his feet and give his English pal a great big hand. Nor was Dave the only one impressed. The Jap general stared at Freddy with the faint light of pleased admiration in his eyes. He presently nodded his head and showed his big teeth in a broad smile so typical of the sly Japs.

"You have the power to move mountains with your voice," he said eventually. "And heartless, indeed, would I be not to give utmost consideration to your plea. I shall see that a few more pieces of silver are placed in Serrangi's hand for selecting you two for the great flight you have made. But Singapore is not everything of importance to us. True, we shall strike at Singapore, and in such a manner that its garrison of troops and pilots will have no opportunity to resist. However, I shall strike at other points, also. It is not our plan to take one place at a time. It is our plan to take all places at the same time. It is the war technique of your own Fuehrer, and it has as yet to be proved wrong. No, we shall not nibble at a spot until it gives away and crumbles. We will strike at many places at the same time."

"*Gott!* Those are words to warm my heart!" Dave cried, and leaned forward eagerly. "And you say, most honored General, that the hour fast approaches?"

The Jap seemed to swell up to the exploding point with indescribable pride and joy. He made some quick motions with his two hands, and although he cried the words out in flawless German his voice had the pitch of a buzz saw going through a sheet of tin.

"Tomorrow when the sun is in the east, the hour will have arrived!"

Dave Dawson

## CHAPTER SIXTEEN
### *Wings of Valor*

As the Japanese air force general's voice died away a tingling silence seemed to hang over the jungle hut like a blanket. Not a man in the place moved. Dave was sure that his own heart had stood still at the sound of the words. Tomorrow morning? Tomorrow morning the Japs were to unleash their dogs of war against an unsuspecting civilized world? Tomorrow, when the civilized world was doing everything possible to maintain the peace with the war lords of Nippon, the hordes and hordes of little brown rats were going to spring savagely at white men's throats? It seemed almost impossible to believe. It was like a dream. Little Japan was going to strike. Little Japan? But there was just another of the white man's mistakes down through the years. Looking upon the Land of the Rising Sun as little Japan. Little in size, yes. But the British Isles are little in size, too, from the standpoint of land area in square miles. Little Japan! That was the trouble. Little on the outside, and tremendously big on the inside. For years and years the Sons of Nippon had been getting ready, and all the time the rest of the world *knew it* ... and *did nothing*. Japan would never strike in the Pacific! No? Well, there had once been the day when, as Germany prepared and prepared, government greybeards and has-beens scoffed at the idea Adolf Hitler would ever take his 1918 beaten country into war. No? Well, where was France today, and Poland, and Norway, and Holland, and all the other "free" countries? Bleeding to death under the crushing weight of the Nazi iron heel. *Little* Japan? Nuts!

"Tomorrow at dawn?" Dave suddenly heard his own voice whispering hoarsely. "It is almost too good to be true. In Germany tomorrow Der Fuehrer will declare a national holiday in your honor, I am sure. Forgive me, but I cannot help but repeat the plea that my comrade and I be given a part, if only a small one."

"Your desire to fight with us, and perhaps die, makes you very eager," the Jap murmured. And an odd note in his voice caused little fingers of ice to grab at Dave's heart. In that moment he had the sudden throat drying conviction that he had displeased the Jap by his pressing insistence. He had the feeling, and the narrow eyed look he received indicated as much, that the Jap general was swaying just a little bit over on the suspicious side.

However, when the little brown son of Nippon spoke again there was nothing in his words or in his voice to justify such a thought.

"But brave soldiers should always be eager to fight and die for their country, and their allies," he said. "And I would not be such a fool as to deny such men their right. You, of course, have heard much of the Burma Road. Through it our Chinese foes had been receiving supplies for many months ... for almost the whole four years of our war of freedom against them. The British did close the road for a few months, but it was just a token gesture to maintain Japan's friendship. And we were not fooled by their stupid gesture for a moment. So, if we smash the Burma Road, China's war effort will starve to death. Her millions will revolt against their war mongering leaders, and throw them to the dogs ... and from then on live in peace and happiness under Japanese rule. And so, it is...."

At that moment the entrance of the little Captain Kito who had come aloft to lead Dave and Freddy down to the secret field snapped shut the General's lips. The chunky pilot shot a swift look at the two R.A.F. aces and then jabbered in lightning speed in his own tongue at his superior officer. Watching the General, Dave saw the man's eyes narrow, and the flaming spark to appear in their depths once more. He saw also the man's claw-like fingers close slowly together as though a human neck were between them. When the pilot had finished there was a moment's silence. The Jap general looked at the two stone faced officers seated at his side and seemed to reach an agreement with them though neither of them uttered a sound. Then General Kashomia turned back to the pilot and sing-songed away for a solid minute. Dave hadn't any idea what it was all about, but he had the very strong hunch that the Jap general was plenty burned up about something and was issuing orders in no uncertain words.

A few seconds later the Jap pilot bowed from the waist and popped outside and down the bamboo ladder. General Kashomia turned his attention back to Dave and Freddy as though there had not been any interruption at all.

"And so," he repeated, "it is of first importance that we cut China's lifeline once and for all, but during the same hour that we strike elsewhere. However, there is a serious problem to be solved between now and our great hour tomorrow. For some weeks, now, a group of fools has been giving aid to the Chinese armies. I speak of what is known as the American Volunteer Group. The aid they are giving China is to patrol the air of the southern end of the Burma Road and attempt to prevent our bombers from reaching it. There are not many pilots in this group of American fools, but they are good pilots, and they have not as yet realized that their task is hopeless. Tomorrow at dawn they will realize the truth at last, but it will be too late, for they will all be dead."

General Kashomia paused and made a little sign of finality with his hand.

"However," he continued a moment later, "word has reached me that the Americans are being reenforced by British planes and pilots. I do not know their strength, but I know it cannot be great because the British have not many planes to spare out here in the Far East. They seem to be more worried about Libya and their own British Isles. Just the same, I do not wish to lose any more of my bombers than I can help tomorrow. The blow I strike at the Lashio end of the Burma Road must be swift and final so that those planes can leave and join the main aerial assault against Singapore, and other points of our attack. Turn your eyes, please, and look at that map, there."

The Jap general stopped talking and pointed a finger at the huge map of Burma, Thailand, and South China, that hung on the wall to his right. Dave and Freddy looked at it and struggled to still the booming of their hearts. In the few moments of silence that lasted within the hut, they heard the sound of aircraft engines being started up outside. Then General Kashomia went on talking.

"To the north of Lashio, on the China border," he said, "is the little village of Pidang. As the crow and the airplane fly it is not fifty miles from here. There in a flat valley, that a blind man could find, is located this squadron of American fools ... and the British who have arrived to help them. For a Japanese plane to fly close to that spot in the light of day would be but the pilot asking that he be sent to join his ancestors. But in a British plane it would all be very different. You would be able to see much, and learn much that I should like to know. Three hours at the most it would take you. And the information you bring me will count much in our success tomorrow."

The Jap stopped short and fixed his folded lid eyes on the two R.A.F. aces. Dave and Freddy returned the stare, and then Freddy broke the silence.

"It is your order, and it will be our joy to obey it!" he cried. "We will leave as soon as your men have fueled our plane, and it is again in working order."

"That is being done now," General Kashomia said quietly. "I knew before I made the request that it would be granted. Yes, at this very moment your plane is being repaired and made ready for flight. But there is time to rest and eat meanwhile. It will be best that you take-off so that your return will be made just before the light of day fades from the heavens. Come! I am sure that the food is waiting, as I am sure you are most eager to fill your stomachs, and quench your thirst."

The Jap senior officer made a sign with his hand and rose quickly up onto his feet. Dave and Freddy scrambled up onto their feet, and then followed the Jap outside, and down the bamboo ladder.

By the middle of that afternoon Dave's nerves were ready to scream aloud and fly off in little pieces. Ever since leaving General Kashomia's hut on stilts he had burned with a great desire to go into a huddle with Freddy Farmer. There was no longer any secret to the Japanese menace, now. At least not to Freddy Farmer, and him. They had heard the story of what was to happen tomorrow from Kashomia's lips. And what the Jap hadn't said, they had been able to guess from unnoticed looks at the maps hanging on the wall. It was to be an all-out air blitz by the Japan air force planned to wipe out Hongkong, Singapore, and the Burma Road all in one fell swoop. By the time the last Jap bomb had hurtled earthward the defenders of Hongkong, Singapore, and the Burma Road still wouldn't know what had hit them.

But the death dealing blow scheduled for tomorrow's sun was simply Dave's biggest worry. He had smaller worries as well, and not the least of them was General Kashomia's plan for them to scout the American Volunteer Group field north of Lashio. That item didn't set well at all, and little fingers of ice rippled up and down his spine whenever he thought of it, which was almost constantly. He had sensed a change in General Kashomia back there in the headquarters hut. It wasn't anything that he could put his finger on, but he knew it was there. The Jap had something up his sleeve, and Dave couldn't dispel the hunch that it was aimed at the life-blood of one Freddy Farmer and Dave Dawson. For Freddy and him to get aloft in the Fairey Albacore again was just too good to be true. And knowing what they did, now, made it seem even more improbable of ever coming to pass.

Yet, everything pointed to the fact that it was. With his own eyes he saw the Jap mechanics refueling the Albacore. And, as a matter of fact, he and Freddy made a minute examination of the plane to assure themselves that it was in good order. The inspection suggestion had been made by General Kashomia himself. But that was the point. That was the one thing that played on Dave's nerves like a rusty file hour after hour. Kashomia was with them every instant of the time. He ate with them, showed them about the secret drome, inspected the rows of Jap war planes with them, and helped them check over their own British made ship. And that was the rub. The Jap never once left their side so that either of them could so much as whisper a word to the other. For all they were able to talk over events to come they might just as well have been at opposite ends of the earth. Whether by accident, Jap courtesy, or devil's purpose, General Kashomia was right there all the time to hear every word that fell from their lips. And so, they had to be constantly on their guard not to let the wrong words drop, and keep them choked up within themselves until they felt that one more hour of the nerve rasping suspense would find them both jibbering monkeys, and stark raving mad.

However, they did not have to endure that one more hour. General Kashomia finally decided that it was a good time for them to leave, and escorted them over to where the Albacore waited with its nose pointed down the tunnel toward the camouflage strip and the open air.

"May your wings have the speed of lightning," he said in farewell. "Observe closely what is there at your objective, and let it be stamped well on your memories. Now, I go to pray to my ancestors that they grant your flight a successful one, and your return speedy."

With a half salute and a half queer little gesture that could mean most anything, General Kashomia turned around and walked rapidly away. Dave shot a thoughtful glance at his back, then shook himself out of his trance, and nodded at the Jap mechanics holding the wheel chock ropes. The little brown rats yanked the chocks clear and Dave fed Jap gas to the Bristol Taurus in the nose, and sent the Fairey Albacore roaring down the man made jungle tunnel. For perhaps two split seconds jungle growth flashed by on all four sides, then the plane shot out into almost blinding sunlight, cleared its wheel and went prop clawing upward.

The instant he was clear and headed toward Heaven, Dave made sure that his radio flap mike was disconnected, and then twisted around in the seat to look back at Freddy. The English youth was sitting like a figure of stone with a beet red face. A thousand million questions seemed to stick right out of the English born R.A.F. ace's face. Dave checked them by a warning gesture toward Freddy's flap mike and waited until the English youth had disconnected it. Then he grinned, tight lipped.

"I know all the questions you're bursting to pop, Freddy!" he shouted. "And my answer to all of them is that we're getting too darn close to being back of the eight ball. That runt sized Jap general is working to pull something very smooth. And it all started when that runt pilot busted in to spill the lingo at him. Check?"

"Of course!" Freddy cried as an agonized look flashed across his excitement and tension flushed face. "I may be all wet, but I think I know why. We pulled a terrible boner, Dave!"

"Gosh! Only one? What?"

"The fight with that Jap sub!" Freddy said with a groan. "I mean, not mentioning shooting."

"The scrap with the Jap sub?" Dave echoed in amazement. "Are you nuts? We'd have been dead ducks in nothing flat if we'd so much as breathed a word about that, you dope!"

"Not the fight with the sub, you balmy idiot!" Freddy roared back. "But we should have said that we were shot at getting away from Singapore. Instead we said that *not a shot was fired at us*! Look out there on the wing. They've even patched that sub's machine gun bullet holes. Don't you suppose they wondered *how* those holes got there? *Why* we didn't even mention being shot at?"

Dave looked out at the ten or twelve little grey fabric patches on the right lower wing, and swallowed hard. So that was why the Jap pilot had come busting in all steamed up. And that's why General Kashomia's face had showed rage for an instant, and why he had obviously barked orders to be carried out. That was the beginning of the change in Kashomia. That was when Dave had felt his hunch that Freddy and he had stuck their necks out just a little too far. That's when....

"That Jap Brass Hat beggar isn't sure of us at all, Dave!" Freddy's voice cut in on his thoughts. "He really doesn't want to know a blasted thing about that American Volunteer Group north of Lashio. This is some kind of a trick, Dave. I'm sure of it. I feel certain that he's sent us up to see if we'd head straight for Singapore. There can't be any two ways about that."

"But what's to stop us?" Dave called back. "My gosh, Freddy, you don't *want* to fly toward this Pidang village, do you? The gas tanks are full, and we can make Singapore easy, and give the alarm."

"Hold it, Dave!" Freddy shouted as Dawson started to level off the climb and veer around toward the south. "Don't try it, yet. There's one thing I guess you didn't notice, or did you? Four of those Nakajima Ninety-Six single seater fighters took off awhile ago, and I don't see them in the air any place."

"So what?" Dave grunted with a scowl. "They probably went someplace else."

Angry annoyance flooded Freddy Farmer's face as he leaned well forward.

"Where's your brains, Dave?" he snapped. "Of course they did! And if you want to know what I think, they went south quite a bit to hang in the sky and wait to see if *we go south, too*. And if you don't think that Kashomia has powerful glasses on us right now, and is in radio contact with those Nakajimas, then you're completely out of your head. So for heaven's sake, let's at least *start* north toward Pidang!"

Dave gulped, blushed to the roots of his hair, and went through the motions of tipping his hat.

"Hail to you, brilliant one!" he said. "Your humble servant is truly one fat headed dope. Sure! You've got something there, and how, Freddy. If we head for Singapore we tip our hand. Kashomia realizes that we're phonies. He radioes his little boys, and the four of them drop down on us to.... Omigosh, Freddy! You are doggone right! That darn Jap rat has fixed us nice!"

"Done what?" the English youth echoed. "What are you talking about?"

Dave didn't reply. Instead he pointed at the empty ammunition boxes that fed his forward guns. They were all empty!

"Good Lord!" came Freddy Farmer's hoarse exclamation a moment later. "So are my guns back here, Dave. We haven't got a single bullet between us!"

"So we darn well do head north!" Dave said grimly and swung the Albacore around. "And maybe, please God, be able to slip around on a detour and slide by those four Nakajimas that are sure as shooting waiting for us between here and Singapore!"

"Amen!" Freddy Farmer murmured, stiff lipped.

## CHAPTER SEVENTEEN
### *Eagles Never Die*

The secret Jap drome hidden deep in the vast jungles of Burma was far behind the Albacore's tail. Still some fifteen or twenty miles ahead was the flat valley floor where the American Volunteer Group, helping to fight China's battle, was squadroned. Dave stared ahead hard for a moment but could see no sign of the flat valley yet. Turning around, he searched the skies with his eyes, but all he could see was eye smarting shimmering light of the burning brass ball in the heavens. Finally, he lowered his eyes, and looked at Freddy Farmer.

"I guess this had better be far enough in this direction," he said and jerked his head back toward the instrument board. "There's enough gas to make it, according to the gauges, but not much more. Do we swing to the east and cut down through Indo-China, or should we swing west and then down south that way? Either way it's going to be close. We.... Hey! Are we *both* dumb this time? What's wrong with the radio? How about contacting Air Vice Marshal Bostworth on the emergency wave-length, and code? The Japs might tune in, but we could at least get things started before they had time to all clear out of there, and.... What's the matter?"

"I didn't think it worth while telling you, Dave," the English youth said in a sorrowful voice. "But my tubes have been removed, and I fancy so have yours. We can't radio anybody, old fellow."

Dave twisted, whipped out his hand, and unsnapped the front of the instrument board radio panel and let it drop down. It was true! Every tube in his set had been removed. For a million dollars he couldn't have broadcast anything as far as the wing tips. For a long moment he glared at the sabotaged set, then he slammed the panel front shut, and squared his jaw.

"Okay!" he got out savagely and booted the Albacore around in a half dime turn toward the east. "We still go back to Singapore, and just let any bucktoothed, throat slitting sons of Nippon try and stop us!"

Brave, determined words ... and they were good for about two minutes only! At the end of two minutes Freddy Farmer suddenly let out a bellow of alarm and pounded a hand down on Dave's shoulder.

"Here they come!" he screamed. "The devils have been riding top ceiling all the time and watching us. Turning off our course was just what they were waiting for. Up there, Dave, to the left! And they're coming down like the blasted devils that they are!"

Dave whipped his eyes around and up just long enough to see a row of four darkish spots against the sun flooded heavens, then he turned his head forward, and kicked the Albacore up, over, and down in a wing screaming half roll. But even as the British plane started to drop the savage yammer of aerial machine gun fire smashed against his eardrums, and out the corners of his eyes he saw the wavy grey smoke of tracer bullets zipping past his wingtips. His heart froze solid in his chest, and the palms of his hands became filmed by a cold, clammy sweat, but there were raging flames of anger in his brain. Anger at himself, at Lady Luck, and at the little brown devils of Nippon.

He should have realized that things had been breaking too good to last. From the very instant Freddy and he had been shot off the Harkness' catapult, Lady Luck had favored them with her brightest smile at every turn. True they had eased into some close and ticklish corners, but they had managed with a bit of luck to ease right out of them again, and continue on toward their big destination ... the secret Jap airdrome, and knowledge of what the Japs planned to do tomorrow. Well, they had reached that secret airdrome, and they had learned of the Jap plans ... but, so what? Dead men can't talk. Dead men can't fly a mile. Dead men would only be buried if they ever did by a miracle reach Singapore. The breaks had stopped, and Lady Luck had turned her face the other way. Death was after them, now, to put an end to all they had accomplished thus far. Death in the form of four war inflamed, conquest crazed Japanese pilots hurtling down out of the brassy sky.

"But not so long as we keep flying! Not so long as we keep flying!"

From as though a thousand miles away Dave heard the echo of his own voice roaring above the yammering guns of the diving Japs. Let the confounded Japs have the guns. Sure, spot them a few guns. Freddy and he would beat them at their own game. There was but one hope. To outfly the Japs and somehow cut away from the rattling death they were dealing out. Given a fair lead the Albacore might be able to keep ahead of the Nakajimas. And with just the tiniest bit of a break....

Dave let the rest slide. Rather, metal messengers of death twanging down through the glass cockpit hatch to practically brush his left cheek caused the rest to clog in his throat. Slamming his strength against the controls he skidded the Albacore sharply off to the opposite side, and then pulled the nose up in a power zoom. For one brief instant wild hope flooded his heart. His trick maneuver had outfoxed the Jap pilots. Too late they tried to haul out of their own dives, but failed and were forced to go shooting on down by the zooming Albacore.

But that hope lived only for an infinitesimal period of time. It died almost as it was born, for not all four of the Nakajimas had piled all the way down. One had remained aloft, just in case. And Dave realized bitterly that its pilot had done exactly the right thing. His three brown rat pals having over shot their mark, he was now blasting down to nail the defenseless R.A.F. plane before it could scoot well off into the clear and build up a lead that could be held all the way to Singapore.

"Lord, if I only had guns!" came Freddy Farmer's rage filled cry above the thunder of the Albacore's engine. "I'd pick that blasted beggar off, even if I had to throw the guns at him. Outfly the rotter, Dave. Outfly him! You're better than a dozen of those brown devils."

It was a nice compliment but Dave hardly heard it. His body was drenched with nervous sweat, and his heart was a battering-ram trying to force its way right out through his ribs. Every instinct of self-preservation within him cried out to wheel away and dive again, but he knew better than to yield to such an instinct. It might spare his own life for a little bit longer, but it would surely spell doom for Freddy Farmer. If he wheeled the plane around he would present a perfect broadside target for the Jap, and Freddy wouldn't stand a chance in the world of surviving the withering fire that would instantly rake the Albacore.

And so, instead, Dave grimly held the Albacore in its power zoom. He sent it thundering straight up into the spitting guns of the Nakajima, until the Jap feared a head-on crash and lost his nerve and broke away. No sooner did the Jap maneuver off than Dave whipped off the top of his zoom, and banked around toward the north. The action brought a startled cry from Freddy Farmer.

"The other way, Dave!" the English youth cried frantically. "We're headed wrong. Singapore is the other way. It's to the south."

"I know our direction!" Dave snapped over his shoulder, and stuck the nose down a shade to pick up all the extra speed he could. "But we'd never make it to Singapore, Freddy. That last burst got the emergency tank feed line, and it's leaking dry. Also those three others would be up to cut us off. Pidang is our only hope, Freddy. We've got to reach that American Volunteer Group, and get them to help."

"Help?" Freddy echoed. "How in Heaven's name? They've only got single seaters in that crowd. Not bombers, Dave!"

"I know that, too!" Dave shouted. "But, they're Yanks. I've got a feeling that'll be the difference. But we've got to get there, anyway, and make a safe landing. Darn these Japs. Whoever said they didn't have anything with speed? Look at them come! Duck, Freddy boy! Keep the old head down!"

As Dave spoke the last he took one last look at the four Nakajimas that were coming after him at comet speed, then turned front and automatically hunched himself down low in the seat. The future was in the lap of the gods, now. Or, perhaps it would be better to say that the future lay in the thundering Bristol Taurus in the nose. If the Japs ever got close again it would be curtains. They had been fooled once, and it was mighty doubtful that they could be fooled again. They were out for blood; out to crush two brave R.A.F. aces valiantly fighting a desperate battle against almost insurmountable odds.

The future? Dave savagely closed his brain to the merest thought. It wasn't the future. It was the present! This very second a lucky burst from those guns yammering like sky wolves right behind the Albacore might snuff out Freddy's life and his own. Might send them hurling down in a ball of flame with the terrible secret of what was to happen tomorrow locked in their brains forever.

"To the left, Dave! To the left and just ahead! There's the flat valley. There's the A.V.G.s'. Base. Just a little bit longer, Dave. Just a little bit longer, and we'll be there!"

Dave heard Freddy Farmer's screaming voice as a distant echo. He had already spotted the small flat valley where nestled the little native village of Pidang, and where the famous American Volunteer Group was supposed to be located. But even as he stared at it hope seemed to die within him. There was not the single sign of a plane, or a hangar on the level floor between the rock studded mountains. Nothing but the cluster of native huts that represented Pidang. Still there must be something else there. There had to be the A.V.G. boys. There just had to be!

Hardly conscious that he was doing so, Dave shouted aloud the words over and over again. And he shoved the nose down to an even steeper angle of dive in a desperate effort to gain an extra foot or so on the gun snarling Nakajimas that were drawing closer and closer for a cold meat kill. If he could only get down and land before they got close enough, maybe Freddy and he could....

He never finished the rest of the thought. At that instant hissing nickel jacketed lead sliced into the cockpit, and a white hot spear of flame ran across the top of his left shoulder. Too late! The Japs had caught up well within range. The next burst would be one that really counted. But in that split second of time before the next burst left the muzzles of Jap guns, Dave put every ounce of his flying skill and daring into savage, furious action. Without so much as a yell of warning to Freddy, he yanked the stick all the way back into his belly and snapped the nose upward so fast that the fuselage seemed to actually bend in the middle and groan in protest against the terrific strain. But that aircraft was English built, and she stayed together. Like a bolt of lightning the plane streaked upward on the first half of a gigantic loop. But before Dave reached the top of the loop he sent the Albacore corkscrewing over to a rightside up position. A half roll off the up side of a loop that brought him out flying in the same direction.

But for only the length of time it would take you to bat an eyelash. Heaving the stick over and kicking rudder, Dave deliberately half rolled again and went plunging down at the vertical. Not until that instant did he release the air clamped in his lungs that seemed to have been locked there for long, long minutes. And he did so with a wild, roaring challenge at the cluster of four Nakajimas starting to zoom up after him.

"Who gives air, you brown rats?" he bellowed. "You or us?"

To the credit of the Japs it must be said that they stuck it out for perhaps one tenth of a second. Then in the face of the flying madman hurtling straight down at them they broke and cut wildly off to the side. One Jap, however, picked the wrong side. One of his own planes was too close to permit room for the frantic maneuver. Two Nakajimas crashed together, locked wings about each other, and exploded in a great fountain of flame. In the nick of time Dave kicked rudder hard and skidded out just barely enough to miss the mass of flaming debris and plunge on down by.

"No guns, huh?" his echo roared back at him. "Brother! We don't need guns!"

Curiosity fought with him to twist around and look back up at the sky, but he held himself in an iron grip and kept right on plunging downward. Two Japs were out of the picture, that was true. But two more still remained. And to look back to see where they were would be only wasting precious seconds. If they were close again, then that would be that. Looking back up into their flame spitting guns would only do harm and no good. It....

"We'll make it, Dave!" Freddy Farmer's joy sobbing voice came to his ears. "We'll make it! You left the two other beggars fanning thin air. They haven't even started down, yet. *We'll make it!*"

Dave didn't give a single sign that he had heard. He was too busy with the diving plane. And the ground was rushing upward at terrific speed. Bracing himself he eased up the nose a few degrees, and gently angled around until he was headed toward the long side of the level floor of the valley. He saw figures rush out into the open, but he had only time for a quick glance, and could not tell whether they were natives or not. Then suddenly he had the plane mushing forward not three feet off the ground. Another moment and the wheels touched, and the Albacore rolled forward to a full stop. Not until that moment did Dave hear the bark of anti-aircraft guns. Not until that moment did he realize that anti-aircraft batteries located in the jungle growth that bordered the edge of the valley were hammering shrapnel up at two Jap pilots trying to get up the nerve to come down and strafe the field. As a matter of fact, even as he threw back his head and looked up he saw the two Nakajimas wheel and go streaking off to the south.

He lowered his gaze to see suddenly the group of sun bronzed American pilots at the side of his plane. One of them was tall and slightly grey, and wore the rank of colonel on his sun bleached shirt. Dave took one look at him, leaped to the ground, and rushed up to grab the man by the arm. Like a man who expects to die in the next five seconds and must get many words off his lips before he does, Dave babbled out the story, all in practically one breath.

"So we've got to smash that hidden drome!" he finished. "Those two Japs will give the alarm to Kashomia, and he may pull out with the whole works for some other place before R.A.F. bombers can get up here. Listen to me! I tell you we've got to do it ourselves. Your gang, and Farmer, and me!"

The Colonel commanding the A.V.G. had continually blinked in amazement as Dave poured out his story. But when Dave stopped talking the senior officer's eye grew cautious, and he stared hard at the two youths.

"That's quite a story," he grunted. "Maybe it's true, but maybe it isn't. You sound a little Yank, but how do I know, huh? And this wouldn't be the first time those slimy Japs had tried to lure us into a trap. About three hundred of their ships hidden down Raja way, you say? Listen, Mister, that's a lot of ships. I...."

Something seemed to snap in Dave's brain, and all went red before his eyes. He reached forward with his two hands, grabbed the Colonel by the shoulders and shook him savagely.

"Listen, you dumb witted fathead!" he ranted. "I don't care what you think I am, but what I told you is truth. *God's truth.* And by this time tomorrow, if you don't do something about it, the whole world will know that you shouldn't even be in charge of flying a kite. A Colonel, huh? You don't seem to have the brains of a private in the rear rank. For the love of God, believe me! But if you won't, you thick headed ape, then for Heaven's sake loan Freddy and me some ammo, and we'll go tackle it alone. Do you hear me?"

The Colonel had pushed Dave's hands free and had them pinned in his own. There was fire in his eyes, but he was grinning from ear to ear.

"You're Yank, right enough!" he said. "Only a Yank would climb a fellow's frame that way. Okay! We get going. There isn't a bomber in the place. But we've got Curtiss P-Forties, and explosive, and incendiary bullets, and.... Haul your crates out, gang! We're throwing a party for those brown devils. And if there's all those crates there, it's going to be some party. Come on! Shift it, you guys! *Everybody!*"

Just six minutes later by Dave's watch he was once more thundering through the sky over Burma. But this time he wasn't in the pit of a Fairey two seater Albacore. He was riding a lightning greased Curtiss P-40. And just off his right wing was Freddy Farmer riding the same kind of ship. Strung out behind were twenty-one pilots of the American Volunteer Group; every one of them spoiling for a fight and cursing his ship on to even greater speed.

Dave twisted his head around to look at them and his heart came near the bursting point so filled was it with pride and joy. He still loved the English boys of the R.A.F., and he always would, for he had lived and died with them for over two years now. But.... But there were Yanks back there, now. Fighting two fisted Yank eagles who didn't care how many of the Axis foe they had to fight, just so long as they could get into the fight.

"Yanks from the good old U.S.A.!" Dave whispered as he turned front. "Gee! I wonder if I'll ever again get the thrill I'm getting now. Those fellows are...."

He didn't finish. At that instant he saw the string of Jap fighters that came darting out from the hidden drome tunnel just east of Raja. They were all Nakajimas, and they started curving up and around the instant they hit open air. Dave let out a war-whoop and fired a short burst from his guns to attract the attention of the others. Then he stuck his nose down and went thundering earthward toward the first of those Nakajimas coming up to give battle. Two seconds later, just two seconds later and the Japs had two Nakajimas less. Dave's guns and Freddy's guns spoke at the same instant and two sons of Nippon went sailing off to meet their illustrious ancestors in an awful, awful hurry. And then, as though by magic, the whole sky over the hidden drome at Raja became filled with twisting and turning man-made air chariots of war. The heavens rocked and trembled with the chatter and yammer of machine gun fire. And the air became a crazy pattern of blazing Jap planes plunging down, and wavy ribbons of tracer smoke that formed a lace curtain in the sky.

Yelling and shouting at the top of his voice, Dave belted and hauled his ship all over the air. And when he wasn't pouring death into some Jap plane, he was hurtling down on the jungle airdrome and raking it from one end to the other with his explosive and incendiary bullets. Perhaps bombers could have done the job sooner, but they couldn't possibly have done it any more thoroughly. Jap after Jap tried to get off to come up at them, but Dawson, and Farmer, and the boys of the A.V.G. slammed them down into piles of raging flames almost before their wheels had cleared.

And then suddenly, a blazing Jap plunging to earth, or a burst of explosive, or incendiary bullets, found the fuel stores and bomb stores of the hidden drome. The air quivered as a great sea of flame came belching up out of the jungle floor. Then sound akin to that of giants tearing off the top of the world closed in on human ears from every side. Dave felt as though his head had been yanked clean off his neck; as though invisible fists had reached down from, heaven to smash sledge hammer blows against every square inch of his body. White fire was in his chest, and his left arm hung numb and lifeless at his side. He tried to cry out but he heard no sound from his lips. The roaring in his brain increased, and a red haze shrouded everything before his eyes.

Seconds, minutes ... years dragged by. He knew that he was still flying the Curtiss P-40. He knew that he was headed toward the north, and that there were other P-40s all about him. He thought he saw Freddy Farmer's anxious eyes staring across the air space that separated him from one of the P-40s. But he couldn't tell for sure. He couldn't force his eyes or his brain to function that well.

Then suddenly the A.V.G. field was below him. He had killed his throttle and was gliding down toward it. He was leveling off and mushing forward. The plane was sinking belly first, fast. It struck the ground, and bounced high. It came down to strike again and bounce. And then the gods slammed a door shut, and there was nothing but silence and darkness all around....

When Dave next opened his eyes it was to find himself under the blankets of an army cot. His chest was taped tight and wound around and around with bandages. His head was also bandaged, and his left arm was in a sling. But his brain was crystal clear, and the only pain he felt was a dull ache in his chest. He stared upward at rough ceiling beams made out of a kind of wood he had never seen before. Sort of yellowish-green in color. Then he saw Freddy Farmer and the A.V.G. Colonel standing at the right side of the cot.

"Just as I told you, Colonel Davis," Freddy Farmer's lips were saying. "Too tough to get seriously injured, this lad. Particularly around the head. Chances are he's been awake for hours, but has kept his eyes closed hoping we'll go away. Always was the one to sleep late. Quite! Lazy, shiftless. You know the type. Oh, greetings, Dave, old thing! You awake?"

Dave glared, then looked at the Colonel.

"Brush that thing out of here, then tell me what's happened, will you, sir?" Dave said. "I guess I crashed, didn't I? But we really finished off those Japs, didn't we? And.... Hey! It's morning! And we went after them just before night. Have I...?"

"Hold everything, Dawson!" Colonel Davis interrupted with a smile. "We wiped out that nest of Japs two days ago. But you didn't crash. You just passed out cold. And you're my sweetheart for bringing that ship down okay. We need every one we have. And, by the by, we didn't lose a plane on that little job. The Jap devils try hard, but they just haven't got the stuff."

"Two days ago?" Dave mumbled as though he couldn't believe what he had heard. "And Singapore?"

"Is still there, Dave," Freddy spoke up. "And by the by, I had a brain wave and Bostworth was able to nab that mysterious spy at Singapore R.A.F. Base. I remembered that Serrangi said ... 'From the very hangars of R.A.F. Base my friend will push the plunger that will....' And he didn't continue. Remember? So after that Jap show ... soon's I saw you had only a couple of scratches ... I got on the radio to Bostworth. He posted triple hangar guards and searched the hangars. Found the detonator, and all the wires leading to buried H.E. Disconnected them all and waited. Next day a young pilot officer was caught digging up the detonator from its hiding place. Been at Singapore eighteen months, mind you. Had even trained in England. Clever blighter, but he's finished being clever."

"And you're kind of clever, too," Dave grinned. "But in a different way. But tell me, have the Japs really gone to war, yet?"

A shadow passed over Freddy Farmer's face. He half turned and looked at Colonel Davis.

"Yes," the A.V.G. commander said quietly. "The very next morning they took several sneak punches at the civilized world. And one of the places was Hawaii, Dawson. An air raid on Pearl Harbor. They did plenty damage, but we'll weather it. But it's really a world war, now. Uncle Sam's in it, now, Dawson."

Dave didn't say anything for a long moment. He stared off into space, as though he were looking eastward across the thousands of miles of land and water to the country of his birth.

"So it's come!" he said softly. "The U.S. is in it at last? Well.... Well, Uncle Sam did it once, and he can do it again, and how!"

### THE END

---

[1] *Dave Dawson On Convoy Patrol.*

[2] *Dave Dawson On Convoy Patrol.*

---

### *A Page from*
## DAVE DAWSON WITH THE PACIFIC FLEET

The U.S. Navy dive bomber seemed to half stop and lurch crazily to the side as the furious blast of fire from the enemy cruiser's guns crashed into it. Dave Dawson had the feeling that he had been slapped in the face with a barn door. Everything turned into spinning red light before his eyes. He knew that he was lashed fast to the seat, that both hands gripped the controls with fingers of steel. But he wasn't sure.

He wasn't sure of anything, any more. Was Freddy Farmer still with him? Was the plane still with him? Or had the withering blast of gun fire from the cruiser below sent him sailing off into thin air and death?

He mustn't die! Not now! The suicide mission had only begun. The aerial torpedo was still in its rack under the Grumman's belly. Or was it? Had the cruiser's gun fire touched it off ... and he and Freddy had failed?

"Freddy! Freddy Farmer! Are you with me, fellow? Are you still there, pal?"

Was that his own voice he heard? That faint little squeak that came back to his ears? If only he could see something besides the dancing balls of red fire. If only he could get his muscles to

Made in the USA
Columbia, SC
20 December 2019